CAROLINE PLAISTED

Piccadilly Press • London

For Nicki who had the original idea
and Jacqui who helped me to get on with it

First published in Great Britain in 2000
by Piccadilly Press Ltd.,
5 Castle Road, London NW1 8PR

A catalogue record for this book is available from
the British Library

ISBNs: 1 85340 676 7 (trade paperback)

3 5 7 9 10 8 6 4 2

Printed and bound in Great Britain by Bookmarque Ltd.

Design and cover design by Judith Robertson

Set in 10.75pt Gill Sans and Keunstler 480

Caroline Plaisted worked in publishing for fourteen years before the
birth of her daughter in 1994. Since then she has become a freelance editor
and has taken the opportunity to indulge in writing. Caroline lives in Kent.

Also available by Caroline Plaisted from Piccadilly Press:

Reality Bites Back!

CHAPTER 1

Wednesday 12 January

Life stinks! I hate my mum, I hate my dad and I hate Billy! And I hate Sally for doing this to all of us. It's because of her that Dad's left us – to live with her – and now we've got to clear out of this house and find another one – a cheaper house – somewhere else. Why should we have to move? We've always lived here. We didn't ask Dad to leave. We didn't ask for any of this to happen. So why do we have to suffer? Some great New Year this is.

It's embarrassing now looking back at that diary entry. Of course I don't *really* hate everyone but what did I do to deserve all this? Maybe if Mum had looked after herself a bit more then Dad wouldn't have gone off and found himself a girlfriend. But then if Dad had spent more time at home instead of at work then perhaps he and Mum would have had more time together and he would have remembered how terific Mum is — brilliant cook, great sense of humour and all that stuff. We used to have really cool holidays, trying new foods, exploring ruins (my dad's big on long walks and looking round old castles and stuff) and just being together.

But hey, you probably don't have a clue what I'm talking about so I'd better introduce myself and explain.

Right. First I'd better deal with me. OK, here's my personal profile – you know, like the groovy stars give in the magazines.

Name: Hannah Davies

Age: 15 – very close to being 16 actually

Home: Just outside of London with Mum and kid brother Billy, who's 13

Hair: Brown, long (very)

Eyes: Blue

Face: OK – occasionally spotty

Best features: Quite tall and slim
My hair (I'm dead proud of it)

Likes: My best mate Kim
Design and Technology (my best subject although I'm quite good at History)
Swimming
M & Ms
Alastair (a dreamboat at school)
My hair

Hates:	Dad not living with us any more
	Watching my mum moping around all day
	Not being in control of anything
	The spots I sometimes get on my chin
	Billy when he's being a total pain (80% of the time)

| Biggest problems: | The fact that my dad left home last year to live with some woman he works with called Sally |
| | My mum being miserable and losing her grip |

You see, last year everything exploded around us when Dad calmly announced to Mum at about ten o'clock one Wednesday night that he was leaving. (I know it was ten o'clock because I've heard my mum tell so many people about it.) They'd been out to a meeting at Billy's school together and gone to the pub for a drink on the way back. Then, there they were eating their supper and watching the news on the television when Dad just finished his meal, pushed his plate away and made his earth-shattering announcement which changed everything. I think that Mum still can't quite believe it and that's why she has to keep on telling people how she found out about it – it's as if, if she keeps repeating it, one day she will understand and accept it.

And Dad did move out that night. The first Billy and I knew was when Dad wasn't there for breakfast next day. It was so unbelievable. Billy and I had no idea that anything had happened, even. But apparently (and believe me I've heard Mum talking a lot about this to her friends) it was relatively calm: no screaming and shouting; no throwing of china and glass. I reckon Mum must have been in shock: she wasn't expecting it – none of us were. So next morning Mum was on automatic pilot – you know, just doing all the things she did every morning only without speaking. Billy kept asking me what was wrong – it was obvious to both of us that something *was*. But I had no idea what – I couldn't explain it to myself, let alone Billy. And I felt really bad because Billy's only young and he was almost crying. I think now that he thought maybe Dad was actually dead.

On the way to school though Mum broke down in tears. She stopped outside the school gate and it was as if someone pressed her 'on' button. She just sobbed. In fact she's been crying now for about a year – in between eating quite a lot of food that is . . . The house has become a mess. And Mum's a mess too. She hasn't had her hair cut for months – and she's going around in sad old clothes that make her bum look really, really BIG!

Anyway. Back to last year. I took Billy in to school and then stayed with Mum all day. Well, it was dreadful. I had no idea what was going on. There was nothing I could do to make

Mum feel better. She wept buckets. Every now and then she mentioned something about Dad but none of it made sense. She was just rambling. Then Nicki rang. (Nicki's my mum's best friend and my godmother.) Apparently, Dad had phoned her and asked her to look after Mum because she was upset! Nicki said she knew what the situation was and that she was coming straight from London. In a way, I was really angry that Nicki was coming. I mean, don't get me wrong: I really like Nicki and that but I couldn't bear feeling so helpless. Nothing I did or said made Mum feel better and I still didn't really know what was going on. And as for Dad phoning Nicki! He's the one who should have been coming home, not Nicki! He's the one who should have been making everything OK!

Anyway, Nicki arrived a couple of hours later and took Mum to one side (in fact, I had to go to my room while she talked to Mum) to try and calm her down. I just sat in my room, feeling my world falling apart around me. I could hear Mum and Nicki talking but I couldn't make out any of what they were saying. But every now and then I could hear Mum weeping and sobbing. It was awful to hear that. The noise she was making seemed to come from deep within her like a kind of moan of an animal in distress. Mums aren't meant to cry – it's kids that cry and mums comfort them. Only in my case I couldn't cry – and I couldn't ask Mum for comfort. And I couldn't even comfort her, could I? I really hated that.

When Billy got home from school that afternoon, Nicki helped us to make tea while Mum stayed upstairs in her room. Nicki explained to us that Dad had moved out and had gone to live somewhere else. She said that Mum didn't really want to talk at the moment but that Mum needed us and really loved us and would always be there for us. I sat there in silence. Billy said, 'When is Dad coming back to see us though?'

'On Saturday,' said Nicki. 'He wants to take you out for a McDonald's and talk to you about stuff.'

And that's what happened. Mum and Billy and me bumbled our way through things until Saturday. Well, Mum spent most of her time crying, either on her own in her room or on the sofa which completely freaked Billy out. So I ended up looking after him, mostly. At least that gave me something else to concentrate on. Except at night when I used to go to bed and just lie there for hours wondering what the hell was going on around here: one minute we were the perfect happy family unit with two kids (or so I thought) and the next we were government statistics – a single parent family! It was awful. It made no sense. And there was nothing I could do to make it better for any of us.

Saturday 15 January
Load of awful people came round the house today. One of them had the nerve to say that they would rip down

the wall in my bedroom and link it with the linen
cupboard! Who cares what they think?! It's our house.

When Dad came to our house on the Saturday, it was really awkward. He just couldn't look Mum in the eye, and she was pretending everything was normal when it very clearly wasn't. It was weird. Then just before we went, Dad called Mum 'darling' and she went berserk! 'I am *not* your darling! Don't you dare call me that!' she said. Dad looked completely surprised. When we got to McDonald's Dad started to explain that he and Mum just didn't get on well any more. He told us how much he loved us and how he would always be there for us, just like Mum, but that it was better for all of us for him to go and live somewhere else. Yeah, yeah, yeah!

Billy asked Dad if he still loved Mum. Dad hesitated for a bit and then he said, 'I still love Mum, yes, only not in the same way that I used to. I love Mum but I'm not "in love" with her.' Billy clearly hadn't taken on board what Dad said. I think he thought that everything was really just as before – that Dad was on some kind of holiday and pretty soon he'd come back and everything would be like it was. Poor old Billy. As if that wasn't bad enough for him, I went and lost it with Dad – in public. I didn't plan it, honestly, but I just let rip and I ended up crying and screaming at him. I didn't let him say much and when he tried to put his arm round me I just pushed him away. Even worse, I'd just got up to run home when I ran smack into Alastair (the hunk at school) as he was coming into McDonald's with his mates! And I was in floods of tears, and my dad was calling for me to come back . . . I must have looked such an idiot! What a nightmare.

And all thanks to some woman called Sally whom I hadn't met – and didn't want to.

Wednesday 19 January

Mum was showing more people around the house when I got home from school. Nicki's told her that you've got to make the house feel homely so Mum had all the open fires roaring, bread warming in the oven and the coffee machine on. It smelt great but I don't think I've ever been so hot or drunk so much coffee in my life!

Friday 21 January

Gross! We had hockey this afternoon and Miss Mason made us carry on to the end of the match even though it was raining! Sadist!

Grosser! Mum's announced that we've got to get the house tidy because there's more people coming to look around tomorrow. I can't stick any more people talking about our loos and whether we've got nice neighbours. Think I'll hang out at Kim's instead.

And I've got a zit on my chin.

I expected Sally to be younger than Mum and much prettier. In fact I got the shock of my life when I met her the first time. She *wasn't* younger than Mum and she *wasn't* prettier. What she was though was more *together* than Mum and, unlike Mum, she didn't (and doesn't) have anyone else to think about other than herself – and Dad, of course. Now, I'm not saying Sally's ugly or anything – it's just that she isn't, well, *special* – drop dead gorgeous or anything. As my gran says, if you saw her in the street you wouldn't look twice at her.

Gran's terrific – she's my dad's mum but she's been a huge help for Mum and us. (My other gran died when I was a baby so Gran's like a mum to my mum too.) She reckons that one of the things Dad thinks is great about Sally is that she doesn't nag at him all the time that the house needs painting or that the car needs a service and there's no money to pay for it. Gran also reckons that Dad's a great big baby who needed Mum to give him more attention than she was able to find the time for. Grown-ups or what? So now Dad lives with Sally, and Billy and I have to go and spend every other weekend with the pair of them.

My best mate Kim hasn't lived with her dad for years. Her mum and dad have this agreement that it is up to Kim to say when she wants to visit her dad and stuff. It seems to work out quite well for Kim. I mean, Kim's into loads of things: orchestra, GCSEs, me, her boyfriend Jake – tons of other stuff. Kim's dad doesn't get stressed if Kim turns round and says that she doesn't want to see him because she's got a rehearsal (she plays the clarinet) or something. Now *my* dad on the other hand doesn't seem to see life like that. Oh no. Oh boy . . . Just after Dad first left, he announced that he and Sally were expecting me and Billy to come and stay with them every other weekend. (When he'd finally admitted that he was living with Sally that is.) Honestly!

Of course, Billy was dead keen to do that. He missed Dad desperately and suddenly here was Dad wanting to take Billy to the football match and to the latest film – all the things he Hadn't Been Able To Find The Time To Do when we all lived together. But there was no way I wanted to do all those things! I mean, when you're at home and stuff you can just hang out and do the things you want to when you want to. There was no way I wanted anything to do with Sally – I certainly wasn't going to go round to her house and hang out with her. No way! How could Dad or Sally have expected me to do that? I mean it was entirely because of Sally any of this happened. So I told Dad to stuff it – I wasn't going. And for about six months I simply didn't see Dad at all. I was so angry with him!

Gran tried to talk me round. She tried to get me to see Dad when he wasn't with Sally but I said no, I wasn't going to see Dad until he left Sally and came back to live with us. So Billy used to go on his own. I even went out or stayed in my room when Dad came round to pick Billy up or drop him off. A couple of times I did take a peek at Dad through the bedroom window when he left. He always looked the same, and that made me mad! I mean Mum was a wreck since Dad had gone – and he just had new clothes on and looked fine! After a couple of months, even Mum tried to talk me round. She said I should at least talk to Dad on the phone but I wouldn't. If he rang and I answered the phone I either hung up or just handed the phone to whoever else was in the room.

In the end, I think I started to see Dad again because of Billy. You see Billy used to get really upset about the whole thing. I couldn't bear to make things worse for him. So I arranged to meet Dad at McDonald's again. It was awkward. I don't think that Dad could understand how I felt about Mum and the way things had happened. Dad seemed to be so pleased with himself about his new life that he couldn't see it from anyone else's point of view. He just went on and on about how he was going to do this and then do that, get a new car, take us on a skiing holiday. He just couldn't seem to get real and realise that Billy and I didn't want to ride around in a new car and go on holiday with Sally. He could stuff his holiday and just give us back our family!

But it has got better as time has gone on. I see Dad every fortnight but I don't often stay the night. Dad comes to get Billy (he doesn't live that far away) and I either go with them or go off and do my own thing and then go on to Dad's house afterwards. Well, Sally's house.

Monday 24 January

Mum was all jittery when I got home from school. The estate agent rang to say the people who came on Saturday want to come and have another look on Wednesday. For someone who wants to sell this house, Mum didn't look that pleased.

Contemplated trashing my room to put people off but I don't think I could bear the mess. Billy's smelly rugby kit might do the trick. Hope there's a power cut when they come!

Had an e-chat with Kim after my homework. Felt better until Mum made me clear the line so that Nicki could ring her. Parents!

Looking back, the first couple of times I went round to Dad's, I behaved *really* badly, Not that I'm sorry though. I wanted that Sally woman to know exactly how much trouble and heartache she'd caused. And the only way I could make her feel that was by taking things out on her. So, when I was at hers, I'd do stuff like pretend to forget her name or just ignore her when she spoke and only take notice if Dad was in the room. Sally was such a wimp though – so irritating! No matter how rude I was, she'd spend all her time trying to suck up to me and Billy – and that just made me worse. Even Billy, who was so desperate to please Dad, gave Sally a hard time. 'This is disgusting,' he'd say when Sally served food. And then Billy would shove it across the table. I'd stare at Dad trying to guess what he was thinking: it was obviously difficult for him (shame!) because I could tell he really wanted to shout and scream at both of us. But I suppose he didn't want to make a scene in front of Sally. Tough! And Billy and I milked it for all it was worth.

It's better now because we've just got used to it, but I'm still not sure that Sally really enjoys having me and Billy dripping around her house anyway. I don't think she understands about hormones and spots. Anyway, it's very much her house (it's all frilly curtains and girly stuff – not at all the sort of stuff that Dad used to like when he lived with Mum). And it's not that big so when Billy and I are there we take up rather a lot of room. There's just about two spare bedrooms for us to stay in when we go there but one of them is really Sally's dressing room ('so posh' says Gran) and you can see when Sally is trying really hard not to get twitchy and not to worry about her pale pink curtains as my oafish younger brother grabs them with his mucky paws. Dad tactfully suggested that I was the one that got to sleep in the dressing room on the basis that I don't always go to stay. So that's what we now do and, if I stay (which I try to avoid as much as possible), I sleep in the pink frills and try hard not to get my mascara on the matching bedspread – not!

The last disaster was when Mum announced that we had to move house. I was so angry! Mum told me about it first – I think she was hoping that I could somehow help her to break the news to Billy because she knew that he was going to be even more upset than I am. But what about me? Why should I find it any easier to move than Billy? I guess we've got no choice: you see the whole Mum and Dad thing has got seriously final. Mum told me that she and Dad are actually getting divorced and that means that all the financial stuff has to get sorted. And that means selling our house. Mum's a bit cut up about it too. She told me last night that she's going to find it really hard to move. She and Dad came here about seventeen years ago, a couple of years after they got married. Mum was crying again when she told me that she had brought Billy and me home from hospital to this house and that she felt that she'd be leaving a part of us behind. It's so sad.

So that's why our house went on the market and Mum's looking for a house fairly close by. It's got to be smaller but in the area so that Billy and I don't have to change school. Mum says I'll be able to do whatever I like to my new room. But I love my old room – *my* room – and I don't want a new one. Thanks to Sally though, it looks like I don't have any choice.

Like I said, life stinks!

CHAPTER 2

'Hi Kim, it's Hannah. I need to talk.' As soon as I said it I realised how dramatic I sounded and pulled an embarrassed face at myself in the hall mirror.

'That bad, huh?'

'Yeah. I can't bear it. I've got to go to Dad's for supper on Saturday. And spend time with that awful Sally. And on top of everything we've got hundreds more people coming to look round the house this evening.' It was those people coming for their second look. 'Honestly, if I hear Mum say just once more that "When we bought the house, there used to be a bathroom in here and that bedroom was only half the size", I think I'm going to start screaming that there's the ghost of a mad woman in the attic and that the garden was originally the site of a graveyard! I need to escape! Fancy some virtual retail therapy?'

Kim and I had spent many hours surfing various websites of some of the major fashion houses and clothing shops.

'Great stuff. I'll get the kettle on and log on to the Prada site. I'll see you in precisely two minutes!' That was one of the many brilliant things about Kim — she lived for the moment and just got on with things. It was one of a zillion reasons why she was my best mate.

Wednesday 26 January

Had a real laugh with Kim tonight: we pretended we were off on a world cruise and window-shopped the net for the clothes. We spent thousands! Kim was talking about Jake. She says he sometimes wants to hang out with her too much. Honestly! She's lucky she's got a boyfriend! But with all this wacky stuff going on in my life, the last thing I need is to worry about a boyfriend as well. Kim doesn't worry: her motto is, 'treat 'em mean and keep 'em keen'. Wish I had her style. Mum didn't say anything about the people who came to the house. Wonder what happened?

Thursday 27 January

I can't believe it! Our house has been sold already! Mum told me when I came home from school today – Billy was there as well and he just burst into tears and went stomping off to his bedroom. Mum tried to go up there but he barricaded himself in and wouldn't let anyone in. So now Mum's really upset as well and she's going on about Dad and how all this is his fault. But no one seems to be worried about me and how I feel about all this! No one's asked me if I feel OK! Mum's already seen a couple of little houses somewhere near to the centre of town. She wants me to go and have a look at them with her to see what I think. We're going on Saturday.

Mum and I traipsed up the garden path of the second of the two houses. The estate agent's particulars described it as 'convenient to all local amenities', which I suppose refers to the '8 till late' shop on the corner of the street. You couldn't get a greater contrast to our house – *our* house, the one we were leaving with its two bathrooms and huge designer kitchen. This one was so small you could have fitted it, garden and all, on to our front lawn. I couldn't imagine Dad wanting to live in it. But then once upon a time I couldn't imagine Dad wanting to be with someone frilly like Sally and that, as they say, is history.

Mum rang on the doorbell and then turned round to peer over the top of her glasses at the rest of the street. I just stood and looked at Mum looking. She was a state. For a start she must have had those glasses ever since Billy started at school. In fact she definitely has because I remember her getting them when she first started working on the *Borough Star* which was just after Billy left nursery school and started 'big' school. Before she had us, Mum worked as an editor on a magazine in London, so when she was able to have more time after Billy started school, she started to work part-time on the local paper and she's done it ever since. I don't think she enjoys it much – she says the editor of the newspaper doesn't think that women have got brains in their heads and only sends her off to report stories about old ladies' cats getting stuck up trees and little kids' Easter Bonnet competitions. Neither of which can really be very exciting. A bit like her elderly glasses. Honestly – what does she think she looks like? The frames on her glasses are HUGE! They cover up her whole face and they are so heavy they keep sliding down her nose and she keeps on having to push them back up. There's a little mark on their bridge where she keeps poking at them. I've told her before that she needs to do something about them but she just says that she doesn't need to because her prescription hasn't changed for years and 'anyway, it's only me and I never have anywhere exciting to go'. She's just so uncool – the woman has no pride. I mean, if she did, she'd lose the weight she's gained and smarten up her act. Get some new clothes. New shoes. Get trendy. Get a grip!

Suddenly, the door was opened and a bloke asked us in. He looked completely weird – like *The Creature from the Cellar* or some other bad horror movie. And I'm telling you, that house was awful too. In fact it was gross, with walls that looked like they'd been painted various colours of sick and a revolting smell of cats (six of them to be precise). We ended our grand tour by yomping our way across the tiny boggy lawn (between the cat poos and the headless garden gnomes – don't ask me why they were headless, I've already told you that this house and the guy who owned it were weird) and then Mum stopped and looked up at the back of the house. I couldn't believe my ears when she said to The Creature that she was very interested in his house. She was? Why? Had she suddenly taken up charity work? Apparently she was going to speak to the estate agent soon. And with that she shook hands with The Creature and walked back through the house and out of the front door leaving me to trail speechlessly behind her.

On the drive home I kept trying to speak to Mum to ask her what on earth had possessed her. But somehow my brain didn't seem to be able to connect with my vocal chords. *I think* I was opening and closing my mouth but certainly no sound was coming out. I must have looked liked a goldfish inside the tank that was my mum's car. Mum however, didn't seem to notice my problem at all. She was jabbering away ten to the dozen about how much potential this house had and how great she thought it could be. How it was really quite cheap so we'd have some money to renovate it and make it look just like we wanted it to.

Had my mother gone completely mad? I mean, how on earth could we possibly make this, this . . . so-called house into the same house that we lived in now? It was half the size for a start and then, on a scale of one to ten using our home as ten, this other house rated at about two – and I am being generous. I was finding it hard to imagine what my mum meant by potential. But she was so full of herself that she didn't even notice that I wasn't answering her. Eventually though she realised.

'Hannah? Is there something wrong? Are you still having a problem with the smell of those cats? You don't have to worry about that – we'll just rip up the carpets and take them to the council dump and then the house won't smell. It'll be fine.'

'Fine?' I croaked. 'Fine? That house will be fine?' I was starting to get angry with Mum now. 'In exactly which way, *Mother*, will that house be fine? When someone else buys it? When someone bombs it? You cannot be serious, Mum! I will not be seen dead going into that house! What will Kim and my other friends say? I am not going to live there and that's final.' I folded my arms and looked out of the car window. Mum was just turning the car into our road.

'Hannah! Don't say "Mother" to me like that! You make me sound like some kind of Victorian old maid.' Mum pulled up in our drive (something else that we wouldn't be able to do at that grotty house) and switched off the engine. She ran her fingers through her hair (which had gone very grey over the last year) and sighed.

'Hannah, do you think I want to leave here? Do you think I want to have to live in a smaller house and spend the next year scraping paint off walls? Well I don't, but I don't have much choice, do I? My solicitor said because of the divorce' – Mum almost choked when she said it, she really was miserable about getting divorced – 'this house has to go. Anyway, even if we could stay in it I simply couldn't afford to pay for its upkeep. Sweetie, I can't do this on my own. I *know* how much you don't want to move and I *know* how miserable Billy is about it too. I need your help, Hannah – to make Billy come round to moving and then to make our new house *our house*. Hannah . . .'

Mum touched the back of my hand and then stroked it gently, just like she always had when I was miserable since as long as I can remember. At first I was irritated – did she think I was some kind of kid? – but actually it was comforting. I still needed a hug every now and then and by the look of Mum maybe she did too. 'Hannah? Let's not tell Billy about that house just yet, shall we? Let's you and I talk about what we reckon we could do with it – you know, spend the million pounds on it that we haven't got? Then maybe we'll talk about it with Billy. Come on,' Mum started to get out of the car, 'Nicki sent me loads of interior design magazines. Let's grab ourselves a coffee and a biscuit and start spending that money now.'

Saturday 29 January
Mum is absolutely serious about it. That house – The Grots would be a good name for it. It turns out she's already taken a builder around the house and had costs done for boring old things like rewiring and replumbing. She reckons that it'll only take us a year and we can get

the house the way we want it. Want it? She has gone
completely mad – barking! She might want it but what
on earth makes her think that Billy and I would want it?
WE DON'T! We want to stay in this house – our house!
Damn Dad and damn Sally! It's all their damned fault!
It's only because of them that we've got to move anyway.

After we'd been around The Grots, Mum sat showing
me all sorts of kitchens and bathrooms in magazines.
She was full of them but she never seemed to
understand that all the kitchens in the magazines were
about seven times the size of the one in The Grots and it
was never ever going to look as good as the ones in the
magazines. She kept going on about how our house used
to look really tatty when I was a toddler and Billy was
just born but then she and Dad had spent loads of time
and only a little bit of money on making it look good.
Well, I can remember being in my pushchair but I
certainly can't remember seeing my mum and dad up a
ladder transforming Domestic Hell into Domestic
Heaven. What is she talking about? I'd better check it
out with Nicki – she's coming round tomorrow. But
tonight I've got to endure Miss Frilly's Thai supper. Gross.

'Sweetie, your mum is just brilliant with a paintbrush!' Over
lunch, Nicki told me all about the zillions of things Mum and
Dad had done to our house. 'You can't believe how

positively *ghastly* this house was before your mum and dad got to grips with it. And your mum tiled the kitchen all on her own. I mean, please – she'd never done any tiling before and now look at this beautiful kitchen!'

Was Nicki really talking about the same person? My mother? *My* mother? I mean my mum hadn't been able to file her nails properly for the last two years let alone file the edges of a tile so that it fitted a worksurface. No, I'm sorry. I couldn't buy this one.

'Don't look like that, Hannah. Anyone would think that you don't believe me!'

'She doesn't!' Mum sort of laughed and started to clear the plates from the table and take them out to the utility area of the kitchen.

When she'd gone through the door, Nicki leaned conspiratorially across the kitchen table and whispered to me. 'Look, Hannah. I know your mum isn't looking and sounding like her best at the moment but believe me – trust me! She's a really talented woman, you know. She's a great editor – totally wasted on that local rag. And when your mum's dressed up she looks really great.' Nicki looked over her shoulder as if she was checking to see if Mum was coming back into the room.

'So what you're saying,' I leant closer towards Nicki, 'what you're saying is that my mum used to be an attractive woman with a busy career and lots of zap?' This was pretty hard to believe. Mum couldn't even organise the weekly shopping any more.

'Of course she was – she still is underneath, you know. Don't look so surprised, Hannah! Your mum really took a back seat after she had you and Billy. She's looked after and loved both of you to bits. She still does! And now that you've both grown up into such great people . . . and now that your dad's gone . . . well, she's just got herself and I think she's a bit frightened about that. I mean, her career's been on hold and I get the feeling that she feels a bit like a woman with three heads – you know, as far as she's concerned, she must be awful if your dad decided he didn't want her any more.'

I rubbed my hands together. I didn't really know what to say to Nicki. After all, maybe what she was saying was true (although it was pretty hard to believe that my mother was as brilliantly talented as Nicki made out) but what was I meant to do about it? I was having a bum time of it myself so how could I help sort it for someone else?

But maybe there was something in it. Maybe Mum could get her act into gear a bit more. Start with the little things – you know, get her hair cut, sort out the glasses – stuff like that. If what Nicki was saying was true, Mum already had the ingredients there, they just needed mixing up again and blending in a different way. A kind of reinvention of the mum that was there underneath . . .

CHAPTER 3

Sunday 30 January

Sally wears a pinny with cutesy kittens on it! Please! Food was OK but Dad was his usual dribbly self with Sally.

Been thinking a lot about Mum re-inventing herself. I'm sure she'd look a heap better if she lost a stone and had her hair cut. Think I'll speak to Nicki about it some more.

My planning was interrupted by Billy coming into my room. Mum had packed Billy off to bed over an hour ago so he should have been asleep by now. Normally I get really hacked off by Billy coming into my room – especially when I'm doing something really private like writing up my diary – but he looked so miserable that I felt sorry for him.

'Hannah, can I come in?' Billy was whispering and half looking over his shoulder down the stairs towards Mum's room. Mum had also gone to bed to read one of her epic novels – since Dad left Mum just seems to read and read and read these days. She says that she's catching up on all the novels she hasn't had a chance to read for the last ten years or so.

'Sure, Billy,' I quickly slipped my diary under my duvet and beckoned him in. He shut the door quietly and slumped down on the bean bag that Nicki had given me for my last Christmas present. 'What's up?'

'Oh . . . um . . . Hannah . . . this house . . .' He was taking such a long time to get the words out it was obvious how upset he was. Billy never seemed to be happy these days. For a split second I really hated Dad for what he was doing to Billy. 'I mean, when are we moving? Where are we going to go?' I could see the tears in Billy's eyes and he looked so sad that I could feel the tears beginning to well up in my own.

'Oh Billy Boy, don't worry about it. I don't think there is a date yet for us to move. You know, all the stuff – the paperwork – is still being done by the solicitor's and we've still got to find a house to move to.'

'But where are we going to go, Hannah? If we move far away then I won't see Rory or my other mates and I'll have to go to a new school and things. And then Dad will probably be miles away as well and we'll never see him.' Billy looked very small – and very worried and very young. I almost wanted to hug him to make everything seem all right but that would have been disgusting so I stopped myself.

'Billy, don't worry too much. We won't be going that far – in fact I think there's a good chance that we'll move closer into town.' I thought of The Grots and wished I could tell Billy about it – but I'd promised Mum that I wouldn't let on about it just yet. I was sure she was right because there was nothing definite about it yet and Billy was upset and messed about enough as it was without telling him about something that might not even happen. 'You won't have to change school, Billy, so you'll still be able to see Rory.'

Billy looked so relieved! Rory was his best friend. They'd known each other just about for ever – they'd been to nursery school together and to primary school *and* secondary school. In fact, it was when they started at secondary school that the pair of them had been separated for the very first time and put into different classes. They were almost hysterical when they found out about it! Rory climbed a tree and stayed up there for three hours. He only came down when his mum asked if Billy would go round to talk him down. Billy did and then the two of them tried to start a petition to send to their new headmaster to make him put the two of them together. They only got two signatures: Billy's and Rory's. So they had no choice and went into different classes but they try to spend as much time with each other as they possibly can.

'So you think we won't be that far from Dad either?' Billy was cheering up a little.

'I reckon so, Billy.' I scruffled his hair a bit and regretted doing it straight away when Billy pushed my hand away. He was thirteen after all – I couldn't keep treating him like a kid any more. 'You'll still be able to go to football with him. All those sorts of things.'

Billy even gave a little smile. 'Yeah?'

'Yeah. Hey listen, you'd better get off to bed or Mum will kill us if she finds out we've been up nattering. 'Night!' I watched Billy open my bedroom door and before he disappeared, I said, 'Mum will find somewhere for us to move to soon, Billy. Wherever it is, it'll be fine.'

Sunday 30 January – midnight

I feel horrible. Now I've lied or at least fibbed to Billy about The Grots. Not only have I not told him that it exists and that Mum wants us to move there but I've also told him that it will be OK. And I'm not sure that it will.

It was break next day before I got to talk to Kim properly. We read the latest issue of our favourite mag and I told her about this disastrous new spot cream I'd bought. Then I filled Kim in on everything that had happened over the weekend: Sally's pinny, The Grots, Nicki, Mum's past ability as a painter, decorator and interior designer, and the reinvention bit.

'I have to say – no disrespect and all that because I really like your mum – but she doesn't really do much with herself, does she? I mean apart from her job and stuff? My mum was a bit like that I think when she and Dad split up, but because she was commuting to London for her job she kind of had to keep herself smartened up I suppose.' Kim was leaning against the wall outside the art block.

'Mum never goes out really. She's gone out with Nicki a couple of times but otherwise she never goes to the movies or to meet up with friends or anything. All she does is sit around reading novels – which is better I suppose than when Dad first went and she sat around weeping. Now the weeping only comes every so often.' I kicked at the tarmac with my feet.

'Hmm. Maybe you could try to prod her on a bit . . . Hey, I've got an idea! My mum and yours get on OK, don't they? They always chat quite happily at school meetings and stuff, don't they? I wonder if I should suggest to my mum that she could go to the movies with your mum? What do you think?'

Just then the bell went. 'Worth a try, isn't it? Nice one, Kim! Thanks!' I picked up my rucksack from the ground and passed Kim's to her. 'Now for exciting double Geography with Dribbly Dobson. Can't wait . . .'

'Yeah, but Alastair will be there, won't he?' Kim gave me a knowing look and I could feel myself blushing. I shrugged.

'Don't look like that, Hannah! I know you still like him! You should talk to him. I'm sure he likes you.'

'I couldn't possibly! There's no way I can even look at him, let alone talk to him, after The Incident.'

'Hannah, don't be ridiculous. OK, so you were in McDonald's and you were upset. And he saw you. It's no big deal. He's probably forgotten all about it anyway. Look, there's a group of people going bowling tomorrow night – Jake told me. I think that possibly Alastair might be going.

Why don't we go too? That way . . .'

'No I couldn't. I mean not on a Tuesday night. Not at such short notice . . .'

'Hannah. Listen to me. Of course you can go. You're not behind on any homework or projects, are you?'

I shook my head. 'But . . .'

'But nothing. Just come out with everyone. Things won't fall to pieces if you suddenly change plans and do something spontaneously for once. And your mum and Billy can cope without you for one whole night. Come on . . . come bowling.'

Kim was right. It would be fine. It might even be fun! I'd been promising to go out with her and her boyfriend Jake and his mates for ages, but had never got round to it. And maybe Alastair would be there. And maybe, just maybe, I would speak to him . . .

'Well . . . maybe . . .'

I psyched myself up to tackle Mum about her life that night over dinner. But when I saw her the shock made me utterly forget it.

'Mother!'

'Yes, Hannah?' Mum looked self-conscious.

'You're wearing make-up!' It was the first time Mum had put make-up on for months – *years*! 'When did you put that lot on?'

'Honestly, Hannah, you talk about me as if I'm some kind of alien from outer space.' Mum's cheeks flushed and her eyebrow twitched a little bit – which was something she did when she was getting angry. Ooops . . .

'I reported on a meeting today, the Townswomen's Guild. There was a woman speaking from a company called Colouring House – she explained that we each of us have a colour palette. Then she picked four of us and we had our colours done and got made up. The woman was quite interesting really, and she gave me loads of information for the article. It's going in the weekend edition of the paper.'

'Wow, Mum – you look so *different* with make-up. Really good – especially the lipstick. You should wear it more often.'

'Well thank you, Hannah – though there's not really much need for me to wear make-up these days, is there? I mean I've got no one to wear it for.'

'Rubbish! Mum – it makes you look good. Brightens up your face. You're important, you ought to wear it for yourself! And for me and Billy. We like to see you looking your best.' I got up from the table. Mum seemed surprised by what I'd just said. 'Listen, I've got tons of work to do. I'd better get on.'

'OK, darling. And thanks, Hannah. I'm glad you like the lipstick.'

Tuesday 1 February

Bowling was brilliant! A real laugh, although Alastair wasn't there. I even got a lucky strike! One of Jake's friends told me about this magazine they've got at his school. They use this excellent graphic design package.

He said I could go along and see it with him! Actually he was quite good-looking – not as great as Alastair though.

Wednesday 2 February

Mum went to an aerobics class tonight! She went off with Kim's mum. I know I should be pleased but <u>they were wearing leggings</u>! In public! They looked like two aliens. Mum's were pink lycra! WHAT WILL SHE DO NEXT?

Thursday 3 February

Mum came back with a very pink and blotchy face last night. Not pretty! This morning she was complaining about her legs aching every time she walks. Think it's put her off taking exercise for good . . .

Friday 4 February

Yikes! Jake's friend Rob rang Kim to get my number! And she <u>gave</u> it to him! What am I going to do if he rings me?

Saturday 5 February

No phone call from Rob – thank goodness. Don't know what I'll say to him if he calls!

Mum went with Kim's mum to the cinema tonight – that new film that's won all the Oscars. I stayed in and watched some dreadful TV movie with Billy. So boring. Wonder what Alastair did tonight?

Monday 7 February

*Rob rang! He's asked me to go along to his school
magazine meeting tomorrow. I didn't know how to get
out of it – so I ended up saying yes. Aargh!*

Tuesday 8 February

*The mag meeting was actually quite fun. The graphics
package was just brilliant. Rob's a good laugh too. He
said he'd ring me when the magazine is printed at the
end of the week.*

Thursday 10 February

*I'm meeting Rob at the leisure centre after school
tomorrow – he'll have the mag. Hope the spot on my
chin goes. And I hope I don't act like an idiot!*

Friday 11 February

*Saw Rob – the magazine was great and they'd even
given me a credit for the work I did on screen. Got a
real buzz from seeing my name in print! I've got a
horrible feeling Rob fancies me – but I don't fancy him!
Even worse – total disaster! I was leaving the leisure
centre with Rob and guess who walked in? Alastair!
Now he'll think I've already got a boyfriend.*

4

CHAPTER

Sunday 13 February

Spent the weekend moping around the house. Billy's been to Dad's. Rob rang again. I nearly died because Mum answered the phone. He asked me to go to the cinema. I was so embarrassed I said no. Think he was offended. Kim gave me a hard time when I told her. Said I should have gone and that I'm a right twit for sitting around waiting for Alastair to ring. I've probably blown it with both of them.

Tuesday 15 February – after school

I know it's something I should have expected by now, and I know that it had to happen but it's still been a terrible shock. AND I HATE IT! Mum's bought The Grots and we're moving in four weeks' time! She's just told Billy – he's run off to Rory's saying he won't come home again. Silly Billy – I don't want to go either but there's not much point in hiding away from it all, is there? Mum's going to take him round The Grots at the weekend and show him his new room. She must be *bonkers because if he's capable of running away <u>before</u> he sees how awful the place is, what on earth does she think he's going to do when he gets inside?*

That old bag Sally has got a lot to answer for!

Thankfully I was going swimming with Kim. So while Mum was at Rory's house, trying to get Billy to come home, I was sharing my trauma with my best mate.

'Bad luck,' Kim always seemed to know exactly how I felt. Maybe it was because she'd been through some of the same things years ago. I wondered who had been able to understand how grotty she must have felt when it was her turn. I couldn't imagine how awful it must have been not to have anyone to talk to about it. She gave me a hug. 'Come on, a good swim will make you feel heaps better – all those endorphins running round your body!'

After our swim, we sank back in our chairs in the café and took slurps of hot chocolate. It was just the thing to get us back on our feet after all that exercise. Kim and I had been trying to come swimming once a week for the last six months. I ran my fingers through my wet hair as I idly watched a woman come out of the health suite that was just off the café. I reckoned she was about the same age as Mum – only slimmer and with sharp, short hair. I wasn't quite sure what went on in the health suite because I'd never been in there but whatever it was, it had given this woman a healthier glow than my mum had that's for sure. There must be something about this health suite in the brochures. I sauntered off to reception and got a few, and Kim and I flicked through them.

'This one's about yoga and spiritual exercise,' said Kim, taking a slurp of chocolate and not sounding at all spiritual.

'Mine's about aerobics classes. They do one called Aerofunk. Not exactly my mother's cup of tea, I feel.' I put the leaflet down and picked up another one called Fit'n'Female. Now this sounded more like it. 'Hey, what do you think of this, Kim?' I started reading out loud to her what the leaflet said. Fit'n'Female was a scheme that offered women-only swimming sessions, aerobics at cheaper rates and beauty treatments in the health suite – so that was what went on in there! It sounded just what Mum needed.

'Hey, I'd quite like to join Fit'n'Female myself, Hannah. Take that one to your mum and see what she makes of it. I might take one for my mum as well. Fancy another chocolate?'

'Nah – after reading about all this exercise I think I'd feel a bit guilty about consuming more calories than my swimming has taken away!' I looked at my watch. 'Listen, I'd better go – I've got some reading to do for English tomorrow and I'm a bit worried about Billy. I wonder if he's gone back home yet?'

' 'Course he has, Hannah. I know the little kid's upset but he'll get used to the idea of the new house soon. Anyway, he'll have to, he hasn't got much choice, has he?'

We set off towards the leisure centre doors and for our journey home. Billy certainly hadn't got much choice – and neither had the rest of us.

Tuesday 15 February – 8 p.m.

Billy was home when I came in. He and Mum were having a chat and I could see Billy's red eyes where he had been crying. I just wish Dad could see him like this. Billy never shows his emotions when he sees Dad. All Dad ever sees is Billy looking happy and laughing because he's so pleased to see him and to be going out and doing things with him. He never sees the little boy Billy who's so sad about not having Dad around the house all the time or the Billy who has to share his dad with some woman who isn't his mum.

I've looked through the Fit'n'Female brochure again. I'm dying to tell Nicki about it – and all the Colouring House stuff!

Mum's left loads of paint charts in my bedroom. She wants me to choose the colour scheme for my new room. I think she's trying to suck up to me because she sees me as being a push-over in comparison to Billy. I'm not – but then as Kim says, I haven't got much choice, have I?

Much later, Mum knocked on my bedroom door. 'Hannah? Can I come in?'

'Sure. I was just finishing anyway.' I closed down the programme on the Apple Mac that Dad had bought me for last Christmas. (Mum said he was trying to bribe me by buying something that he knew she couldn't afford – especially a Mac rather than a bog-standard PC, but then Dad had bought it because he said that Macs were the thing for people who wanted to do design work.) I was working on an idea for a new type of shampoo bottle for Design and Technology and I reckoned I'd gone as far as I could get with it that night. 'What's up, Mum?'

'Oh nothing – well at least nothing more than usual. Billy seems to have calmed down a bit. I've been telling him about his new bedroom. Can you believe he wants to paint it black!' Mum laughed as she started to clean up her glasses with her baggy old jumper.

'Black! How on earth are you going to persuade him otherwise, Mum?' Trust Billy to be so stupid.

'Oh I'm not. If Billy wants to paint his room black, he can. I don't care – I won't have to sleep in it. Then if he realises that he hates it after it's done, then he can't blame me, can he? To tell you the truth, I'm getting a bit fed up with being the one who gets blamed for everything that goes wrong around here these days.'

Mum looked tired and I felt a sort of sick feeling of guilt. She did have to carry the can for everything around here now. From the washer going on the kitchen tap the other day, to

Billy running away and having to be calmed down.

'Sorry, Mum. Guilty as charged.' I clicked off the state-of-the-art worklamp on my desk (another guilt present from Dad – did he think I didn't realise what he was up to?).

'Oh no, Hannah – I didn't mean it like that. It's just that – well there's so much to do round here. It's not your fault, sweetheart. Anyway, what I came to ask was whether you'd had a chance to look at the paint brochures I left you?'

'There's one I like in here,' I handed her the brochure.

'Let's have a look. Oops –' Mum took it and as she leant over the other brochures slipped on to the floor.

'What's this, sweetheart?' Bum! It was the Fit'n'Female brochure! Mum put her glasses back on to read it. 'Hey, this was the thing that Pam was telling me about. You know – Rory's mum.' Mum started to flick through the brochure.

'Pam? What, you already know about it? How come?' This was a bit spooky!

'Yes. Pam's thinking of signing on for it – apparently they are doing a special offer of three months' cheap trial membership and she wondered if I might like to go along with her. But there's no time and no money.' Mum laughed. 'And as you know, the aerobics didn't really suit me.'

For the second time in as many days I was speechless. Yesterday Mum had lipstick on and today she was talking about keeping fit. Where was it coming from? But from the back of my throat I tried to grab my voice. I wasn't going to let this opportunity slip through my fingers completely.

'But why don't you join up for the special offer like Rory's mum says? Go for it. How much does it cost?' I grabbed the brochure from her hands and flicked to the bit at the back about cost. 'Sixty pounds for three months. Go for it, Mum!'

'Sixty pounds is a lot of money, Hannah. I probably ought to save it to spend on the new house.'

'Oh come on, Mum. You never do anything for yourself. Go on – join Fit'n'Female.'

'Maybe . . .' Mum stroked my cheek affectionately. 'Listen, Hannah. It's late. You've got school tomorrow and I've got to go to work. Some woman has just opened up a new homeopathic clinic in town and I'm going along to interview her about it for the paper. 'Night, sweetheart.'

'Yeah – 'night, Mum.'

It was only after I'd had my bath and was turning out the bedside light that I realised Mum had taken the Fit'n'Female brochure with her. So the interest was there, I just had to get her to join up. How? I knew! That was it – I'd call Gran and see if we could arrange for it to be Mum's birthday present!

I rang Gran at the first opportunity and told her my idea.

'I think it sounds brilliant, love. You know, when your dad first started going out with your mum she was just gorgeous – quite the most attractive girl he'd been out with. Tell you what, I'll ring your mum up and ask if I can pop over on her birthday. Then I can give her a cheque. We could do lunch for her – what do you think?'

'Brilliant, Gran. It'd do her good to be a bit spoilt.' I was sure that with just a little help Mum would really get into this fitness thing. It looked like the reinvention was about to begin.

'So – seen Alastair lately?' Kim and I were walking home from school. She still thought I was a fool for turning down a date with Rob. My cheeks flushed.

'Well – only in school. You know.'

'Yes, I do. Honestly, you're an idiot! If you ask me it did Alastair some good to see you with someone else. If he's interested in you at all it should make him jealous!'

'You think?'

'I know so. But look, Hannah, life's about more than hanging around waiting for some boy to call. Play the field a bit. You're not going to meet anyone sitting at home.'

I didn't know what to say. Kim was right. But supposing I'd gone out with Rob that night and he'd made a pass at me – tried to kiss me even! What would I have done then? No. I wanted to be in charge of the situation, so I couldn't run the risk of getting into a snog with a boy I didn't even fancy.

Friday 18 February
Nicki phoned today before Mum came home. Apparently one of the people she works with wants to commission

an article about losing weight with a diet club for a feature in a new health magazine – and she thought Mum would be the perfect person! It's funny, I know that Mum works for the local newspaper but Nicki referred to her as a journalist! Mum never calls herself a journalist.

Anyway, Nicki's friend is going to ring Mum and ask her if she'll do the article for her. Could be just the incentive Mum needs.

Alastair smiled at me when we came out of Assembly this morning . . . !

Saturday 19 February

In a way it's a bit exciting about moving to a new house. I mean The Grots is small and in a grotty place and stuff but on the other hand, Billy and I have never had a say in anything about the house we live in now – our <u>old</u> house. Everything had already been done or chosen for us. Dad hates bright colours and bold patterns so everything is very tasteful and kind of <u>controlled</u>. I don't want a black bedroom myself but I have to admit that having a brother who's going to have one is cool. And Mum keeps on asking about what sort of kitchen we'd like to have and if we thought a bright yellow bathroom would be good. Mum seems to really want our opinion and input. Maybe it won't be quite so bad after all.

Sunday 20 February

Mum's birthday! Gran came over to have lunch with us (she stayed for tea as well) and we spoilt Mum for a change. Billy and I did all the cooking (with Gran's help) – we even made a cake! – and we made Mum sit back and put her feet up. Billy gave Mum a pot he'd made at school. It was shaped like a fish – I have to admit it was pretty good. Mum was ecstatic about it and said she'll put it in the bathroom at our new place. I gave Mum a scarf I'd found at a charity shop. It's silk and exactly the colour that woman told her she should wear. Mum really liked it, and it looked great on her. Gran gave Mum a cheque and explained how she thought she might like to spoil herself with it. I went on (probably too much) about how I thought she could join Fit'n'Female. Mum was really embarrassed about it and said she couldn't possibly take the money because it was too much – too generous, she said. But Gran insisted that she kept it to spend on herself. In the end, Mum said she'd keep it but only on the understanding that she could spend it on the new house. I give up!

CHAPTER 5

I was working at the kitchen table when Mum came home and told me that she'd visited the homeopath – you know the one she'd been to see for the newspaper article? I offered to make Mum some coffee but she told me she wasn't allowed to drink coffee any more. My mum – the one who drinks strong coffee at every opportunity!

'She asked me if I had a problem with sleeping and some other questions about my health – but it was as if she knew that I hadn't been feeling great lately. So, she's given me some homeopathic medicine – remedies she calls them. She looked so well herself she was an inspiration! The only down side is that I've got to stop drinking coffee and I'm not allowed to have mint either.' Mum dug around in her bag. 'Look, I've got to use fennel toothpaste.'

I took the toothpaste from her. 'Weird. Still it sounds like she was interesting, anyway.'

'It was – *she* was. Anyway, you can read about it in my article next week. I spoke to her about your spots, Hannah, and she said she'd love to see you about them.'

'Thanks, Mum, for talking about my spots with a complete stranger!' The cheek! (Actually, the spots *were* on my cheeks.)

'I'm sorry, darling, it's just that she was really inspiring. Anyway, that isn't all that's happened to me today!'

'Oh?'

'No. I had this call from some woman that works with Nicki. She wants me to do some research and write an article on a local slimming club that's just started up. It's going to be a freelance job – and I might get to lose a little bit of weight at the same time.' Mum pulled her jumper down over her thighs self-consciously. 'Problem is, how am I meant to have time to do the extra work and move house? And try to diet?'

'Oh Mum – 'course you can. Billy and I will help you with the new house. You know we will. And we'll do all we can to help you with the diet. Promise.' I gave Mum a hug.

'Oh, I don't know, Hannah. We'll have to see.' She looked at her watch. 'Hey, look at the time. I'd better go and fetch Billy from his swimming lesson. That's something else that will be better for all of us when we move.' Mum grabbed her car keys and made for the back door. 'We'll be right in the middle of town so we'll be able to walk everywhere – including Billy who can be more independent too and start making his own way home. See you in half an hour.'

And she shut the door. That was it then. Mum was going to reinvent herself if it was the last thing I was going to do.

Monday 21 February

I saw Alastair in the lunch queue today. He smiled at me again! Wonder what it means?

I met Kim at the school gate the next morning. She was amazed to hear all about Mum's latest plans. But then she had a surprise of her own.

'Apparently our mums met up again the other night. And they were talking about the choral society my mum belongs to. And it sounds like your mum's been meaning to join a choir for years – she used to sing when she was younger – and so tonight, your mum is going to give it a whirl and think about joining. Apparently it's all been arranged for days.'

'You have to be joking!' It was amazing! My mum was getting a life. But how come she hadn't told me?

'Kiddo, I kid you not! Tonight, your mum and mine. How about that!'

'Morning, ladies and gentleman.' Mr Chisholm, our form tutor had come in. 'Places, please – it's register time again. Come on – spit spot!' Another school day had begun.

Thursday 24 February

Not much time to write in my diary this week – been snowed under with projects for school. Also decided I need to start revising for the exams, so Mrs Isis helped me draw up a revision timetable. Kim thinks I'm a

*complete swot and just laughs at me. But at least I
know where I am and can tick things off as I go. Just the
way I like it. Still doesn't mean I'll pass, though.*

Saturday 26 February
*Eeuch. Had to go to Dad's house (well, Sally's house) for
lunch. So boring – but at least I could use my revision
timetable as an excuse not to have to stay for the whole
weekend. Said I had too many books to take over there –
which is true really. Sally asked me to go with her to
fetch something from the shops. <u>Please</u>! Even worse
– Dad insisted on driving me home and he pulled up at
the traffic lights next to Alastair who was on his bike.
Alastair smiled and waved at me! Disaster! I mean, how
could I wave back when I was with Dad? So now
Alastair probably thinks I don't even like him! I'm never
going to get off the ground with Alastair, am I?*

Tuesday 29 February
*Mum's still not drinking coffee. And she's been out and
bought a track suit and trainers . . . I haven't seen her
wearing them though. I mean, honestly!*

Thursday 2 March
*Seriously fed up. Saw Alastair at school today and he
didn't even look at me. Probably because of Saturday in*

the car. Even Kim wasn't very sympathetic – she said one minute I give him the come-on and then I cold-shoulder him. She's right really. Drowned my sorrows in my revision.

Saturday 4 March (Half term!)

Went for a swim but Kim didn't come with me because she was at orchestra practice. Saw Jake there – with Rob! He ignored me. Now I know how Alastair must have felt. Kim came round this evening to watch a video of the latest Julia Roberts film.

Mum went out – she said she was going to the cinema. But she wouldn't let on who she was going with. All she would say was a friend. Kim said she was probably going on a date but I told her she must be mad. My mum? Really . . .

Tuesday 7 March

Only two days until we move! Mum has made us do a huge sort-out of all our stuff. It's so much smaller than this place that we just can't take everything. And she says there's no point in taking our rubbish to The Grots and putting it in a bin there. I sorted out tons of old clothes and books and took them to Oxfam. Silly Billy is making a real meal out of it all. Refusing to throw out all his old Playmobil people, if you please! I mean <u>how</u> old is *the boy! Three! Seven! Nine! No – thirteen! When was the last time he played with them! Mum's told him to have a good think about it and suggested that perhaps Rory's younger brother might like to have them to play with. That way Billy still knows where they are and can play with them when he's at Rory's house. I think that did the trick – quite clever really.*

I heard Mum up in the loft this morning. I don't think she realised I was in because she was having a real old sob to herself. She was sorting out all our old nursery furniture – the cot, our pushchair and stuff. She took it all off to one of the charity shops in town.

Anyway, she's gone off to choir tonight – at least that cheered her up. So I'm left to babysit baby Billy.

It was Wednesday night and the day before the packers arrived to parcel up all our stuff for the big move. Mum had just announced that she didn't have time to go to slimming club.

'Why not?' I said. She'd been for the last two weeks and had already lost half a stone. OK, so she had another stone to go but she seemed determined to stick to her diet.

'Well there's just so much to do here. I'd better get on with sorting.' Mum put her herbal tea down and pushed her glasses up her nose. Those glasses! I had to get her to do something about those soon!

'Sort what, Mum? The packers are doing everything

tomorrow and you've got everything ready for them – there's nothing to do till then!'

Mum looked at her watch. 'No, darling. Honestly, I've left it too late for tonight. The session starts in fifteen minutes' time.'

'And it will take you about sixteen minutes to drive there! Go on, Mum. Get to that club – Billy and I want to know how much you've lost this week, don't we?' I gave Billy a great kick under the table.

'Oww! What have I done now?' Billy glared at me, nostrils flaring like they always did when he thought he was in trouble.

'Don't we, Billy? Say yes!' I hissed. Honestly, younger brothers could be so thick sometimes. Billy didn't have a clue what I was talking about – to be honest, he couldn't care less whether Mum lost weight or not or if she had a life as long as she was there for him when he needed her – which was still surprisingly often despite his age.

Billy was still rubbing his shin. 'Yes!' he snorted and carried on with his homework.

Mum looked at her watch again and I leaped into action. 'Here,' I said, 'car keys, coat. Get going and we'll see you later!'

'All right, all right! I'm off!'

Wednesday 8 March

Billy was a complete pain tonight while Mum was out!
He kept on moaning because the television has been

packed. I suggested he did something useful – like going to play in the road. Then he said, 'Why don't you go and do something more useful, like pick your zits? Then Alastair won't have to look at them!'

I nearly died! How did Billy know about Alastair? And did Al count my zits? I must speak to Kim!

Anyway, we move tomorrow! Can't remember living anywhere other than this house. I'm scared and sort of excited as well. Dad rang this evening when Mum was out. He virtually ignored the fact that we're moving tomorrow and spoke about it as if it had nothing to do with him. Perhaps he's got a problem with it – I mean, once this house has gone so has the last trace of our little family unit thing, even though he hasn't lived here himself for over a year. (And even though it's his fault anyway!) I've arranged to see him at the weekend. I'm going there for lunch on Sunday.

Mum came home from slimming club all excited. She's lost another two pounds. She was dead chuffed with herself. I'm pretty chuffed with her too!

'Hannah? Hi, it's Kim. So how goes it in The Grots?' It was Sunday morning and we'd spent two nights in our new home. There were empty packing cases everywhere and the garden was a mass of packing paper.

'Exhausting! I can't believe it – it's so much work. Even

53

with Gran helping we spent all day yesterday unpacking and we've still only done a tiny bit. We're just trying to fit everything in and Mum's burning these brilliant scented candles to get rid of the smell of those damn cats!'

'Poo! Are they working?' Kim *hated* cats. In fact, I think she was really scared of them but she never really admitted it. She just said that she hated them and preferred dogs.

'Sort of. So how's life with you?'

'OK. Actually, it's not that OK. Jake and I had a big row yesterday and now my orchestra practice has been cancelled.' Poor Kim – she and Jake had been going through a bad patch I knew. But at least she had Jake – I just had to put up with admiring Alastair from afar. 'I was wondering if I could come over and help with your new room?'

'Yeah – that would be great.' Kim hadn't seen the house from the inside yet and it would be good to show her. 'Listen, I'm sorry about you and Jake. Oh no! I completely forgot!'

'Forgot what, kiddo?'

'It's Sunday, isn't it? Dad's coming to pick up me and Billy and take us for lunch. Sorry, Kim, I'm going to have to stand you up.' I felt doubly bad because I didn't think Mum had remembered about us going to Dad's. And I reckoned she was going to feel a bit abandoned in the house on her own.

'Oh balls, Hannah! Oh well, never mind. You have a lovely lunch with pally Sally and tell me all about it at school tomorrow. See you later, honey.'

'Yeah — 'bye Kim. And I'm sorry about this.' Kim hung up. The great thing about her was that she never bore a grudge — and she always seemed to understand if you made a genuine mistake, and didn't take it out on you.

I really did feel bad when I reminded Mum about the lunch. I'm not sure if she had really forgotten about it or whether she had put it to the back of her mind and hoped that Billy and I might change ours about going. It was obvious that, even though Mum never stopped us from going to see Dad, she still didn't like us being there. I think it wasn't so much that she minded us seeing Dad, but that she really didn't like Sally being there with us.

'Oh well, sweetheart,' Mum sighed. 'I've got plenty of work to do in the kitchen and it will give me a good excuse not to have to cook a meal. Now, I think I'm going to tackle that mountain of paper in the garden and somehow get it under control!'

Mum went off with a smile on her face but I don't really know how deep the smile went.

Dad came and got us late in the morning. Billy wanted to show him all round the new house. Honestly, he's so stupid — doesn't he realise how difficult it was for Mum to have Dad shown round our new home? After all, he's never going to live here, is he? And Mum hasn't mentioned it but Gran told me yesterday while we were unpacking that two days ago Mum and Dad's divorce came through. So that's it then. My mum and dad aren't married any more.

Sunday 12 March – 11.50 p.m.

Should be asleep because I've got school in the morning, but I've just got to record the fact that Kim is the best friend in the world. And her mum is the best best-friend's mum in the world too! Billy and I came home from lunch to find that Kim and her mum had come round to the house with a picnic lunch which they ate with Mum before they helped her to unpack the contents of the dining room! There's hardly a packing case left with anything in it and Mum seemed really pleased with everything. So I felt much better about having been to lunch with Dad.

Biggest surprise of all was that Sally gave Billy and me a present each for our new bedrooms. Billy got a bedside lamp like a globe. She gave me a new bedside lamp as well – it was all wrapped up and I was dreading opening it because I thought it'd be some ghastly gingham thing with lace on it. But it wasn't. She'd bought it in Ikea and it's quite cool. I didn't think Sally could do cool stuff. I won't tell Mum though that it's from Sally – better if she thinks it's from Dad. I'd better warn Billy to do the same.

And Kim says that Billy was just winding me up about Alastair and the zits because a) I haven't got that many

and b) she doesn't reckon Alastair has noticed them
anyway. Hope she's right.

On Tuesday night, Kim and I went swimming as usual – only, instead of me going home first and then meeting Kim at the leisure centre, we both went along to the library to do some work there and then went on to the pool a little bit earlier than usual. This was because Kim wanted to avoid Jake, who we usually saw at the pool with his mates. The pair of them were having what Kim described as 'a cooling off period'. Quite frankly, I couldn't understand what that really meant because Kim had always seemed pretty cool about being with Jake anyway. I know that if Alastair was my boyfriend I wouldn't be nearly as laid back as she was – I mean, she made Jake just fit in with the rest of her life and I was certain that I'd be the other way round with any boyfriend of mine. With Alastair – if only he'd ask me out.

Anyway, when we got to the centre it was the 'Ladies only session' and the changing room was absolutely packed.

We headed straight for the deep end: we had this dare that we started up years ago about jumping straight in rather than breaking ourselves in gently.

Kim went into the water first and started swimming off. I was trying to catch her and had nearly made it when some woman came ploughing into me. I lost my stroke and floundered in the water a bit.

'Oh, I am so sorry!'

'What do you think you are doing?' I spluttered as I spat out some of the water I'd taken on board. I gave the woman a hard stare. 'Mum! What are you doing here?' It was my mother! Swimming! *In public!*

'Oh, Hannah! Thank goodness it's you!' Mum started to tread water and get her breath back. Kim swam back to where we were.

'Hey, are you two OK?' Other swimmers were beginning to crowd round us a bit — not because they were concerned about our collision but mostly because we were in the middle of what was obviously a busy piece of water. 'Look, let's go over to the side so that you two can catch your breath.'

We just followed Kim as she instructed. Mum grabbed the side rail with both hands.

'Phew. Hannah darling, are you all right? I'm so sorry about that. I just didn't see you without my glasses on.' Mum looked embarrassed.

'I'm fine, I think. But Mum!' I looked at her accusingly: 'What are you doing here?'

'For goodness sake, Hannah. What do you think I'm doing here? I'm swimming of course!'

'But you never go swimming! *Ever!*'

'Does that mean I'm never allowed to? Admittedly, I haven't been swimming very much in the past few years but does that mean I can't if I want to now?'

'But Mum — everyone can see you! Some of my friends might be here!' I wiped a stray bit of hair out of my face with my hand as I said it.

'Hannah!' Kim and my mum both said it at the same time. At first, I didn't understand what they were getting at.

'What?'

'Hannah, please don't speak to me like that!' Mum looked really angry. She sounded angry too: you could always tell when Mum was angry because she spoke in a low and much quieter voice rather than shouting like other people did. 'I'm sorry if I cause you so much offence, Hannah. I wouldn't want your mother's body being seen in public to make your social life suffer. Clearly, I'm not entitled to a life like your father is, Hannah. Right. OK. I'm off. Goodbye, Kim.' Mum started to swim towards the steps. 'I expect I'll see you later, Hannah.' Mum gave me a cold stare and then she was gone.

'Oh my God, Kim, can you believe that?'

'No Hannah, actually I can't.' Kim gave me a funny look which I didn't understand.

'Look at her. She's showing off all that cellulite in public! Doesn't she have any shame at all?' I mean I know I was all for Mum getting her act into gear but really — couldn't she go off and do it in that other world that parents inhabit? I mean she wasn't supposed to take her clothes off in public where my friends might see her! This reinvention was getting out of control. And you know how I feel about control.

'Hannah!' Kim was beginning to shout at me. 'For heaven's sake! Give your poor mum a chance! OK, so she's got some cellulite, but show me a woman of her age in the pool that hasn't! It's not as if she's got that much anyway – there's plenty of other women in this pool who've got more.' I was shocked. Kim had never spoken to me like this before. 'Take a good look at your mum, Hannah. She's lost quite a bit of weight, you know – probably nearly a stone, and she's looking much better than she has for a long time. Have you ever thought of telling her that instead of constantly telling her how ghastly she looks? It must have taken a lot of guts for her to start coming swimming. I think it's great that she's started doing these new things. You can't just have a go at her you know!'

'I – I –' I couldn't think of anything to say. Kim was right. I had been awful. Mum was just getting her confidence back and starting to enjoy things. And it was brave of her to come. And I had been really unkind to her. I looked at Mum as she reached the other side of the pool and entered the changing room. Kim really was right, Mum had lost a bit more weight than I had realised. I mean, I had noticed that her clothes were a bit baggier but they were the same old boring clothes. Now I felt awful: not only had I been unkind about her being at the swimming pool but I had been so wrapped up in myself that I hadn't even noticed that she had lost so much weight. After all, she probably wasn't that far off her 'goal weight' as she called it. Kim looked daggers at me.

'I'm off for a swim now, Hannah. I'll see you in the changing room in about twenty minutes time.' And she swam off without waiting for me to answer.

I felt angry: with Kim, Mum and myself – but mostly with myself. Bum. I'd have to apologise to Mum when I got home. But how? I tried to think of it as I swam methodically up and down the pool. I didn't have a clue what to say.

Kim was still pretty unapproachable when we got into the changing room. In fact, we dried off in silence and then headed for the exit. There was no suggestion that we go for a hot chocolate that night. She turned to me just as we were about to go our separate ways.

'Hannah, I'd think carefully about how to say sorry to your mum if I were you. And I'd think before you open your mouth in future too. See you tomorrow.' She gave me a dismissive wave and was off.

'Yeah – goodnight, Kim.'

Then Kim suddenly turned back to me.

'Come on, hug time.' Kim gave me a bear hug. 'Look, sorry I gave you a hard time but you know you were just awful to your mum.'

'I know.' I hung my head in shame. I could do with another hug.

'Go on – go home and say you're sorry.'

CHAPTER 6

The gate clanked as I opened and closed it. The Grots is so small that, even without the tell-tale noisy gate, there was no way I could slip inside the house without Mum knowing I was already home. She was in the living room sipping at one more of her cups of Earl Grey tea.

'Hi,' I smiled half-heartedly. I think I was hoping that somehow Mum wouldn't still remember what I'd said back at the leisure centre and that she would welcome me back home with a grin and hug. Unfortunately, she didn't.

'Evening.' Mum took another sip at her tea and then flicked over the page of the magazine that she was reading without looking at me. Her lips were closed so tightly together that they were almost biting each other. Billy was sitting in the corner of the room playing with his GameBoy. He hadn't got a clue what was going on.

'I was going to make myself a cuppa,' I said rather weakly. 'Anyone else want one?'

Billy, of course, ignored me and Mum didn't look up from her magazine when she said 'No thanks'. So I went into the dismantled kitchen and switched the kettle on. Mum had had all of the old kitchen completely ripped out and the walls had been mostly replastered or at least massively retouched. Nothing could be done until it all dried out.

I found a mug and rinsed out the builders' dust before I made myself a coffee and went back into the living room and sat down on the chair opposite Mum.

'Did you enjoy your swim, then, Mum?' OK, so it was a pathetic thing to say.

Mum just looked at me, said nothing and then went back to her magazine. There was a silence for a couple of seconds before Mum muttered, 'Well, what do you think?'

I put my coffee down. 'Oh Mum . . . I mean . . . Oh . . . Look, I'm sorry. I really didn't mean it. Honestly. It's just that . . . well, I wasn't expecting you to be there or anything. You never mentioned that you were going to be there. I didn't even know that you went that often. I mean, I didn't think that you'd have a costume that would fit now that you've lost so much weight.' I was pleased with myself for saying that – and it was true anyway.

I was right. Mum warmed up a little. 'Well, actually, I've been wearing my old costume. It's very old but I haven't been able to get into it for a while. And now I can. I usually go on Wednesday mornings. It's part of that Fit'n'Female regime.' Mum flicked over another page. 'The one that you and your gran were so keen for me to join. Once upon a time . . .'

'Well, that's great, Mum. I've been meaning to say,' – *you liar*, Hannah! – 'how much weight you've lost. You must be at your target weight now, aren't you?'

'No.' Mum put the magazine down and then pushed her glasses back up her nose. Honestly, those glasses! 'I've lost ten pounds though. I've got another ten to go.'

'That's great, Mum!' I really meant it. 'Just think, then you'll be able to go out and buy loads of new clothes.' Now that would be good, to get Mum out of her old tat.

'Well, maybe. Come on, I don't know about you, but I'm hungry. Billy? Do you think you could tear yourself away from the GameBoy?' Mum waved her hands in front of his face as if she was trying to make him focus. 'Come on! I've made a new recipe from the diet club cook-book to try. There's even a pudding.'

Obediently, I went to help Mum. I reckoned that I'd got off very lightly.

'Don't worry, Mum,' I said, 'I'll lay the table for you and then come in to help you serve up. And Mum, I'm really sorry about earlier . . .'

Tuesday 14 March

Nightmare day! I still feel absolutely rotten. I was rude to Mum in the pool and I showed myself up in front of Kim – and she obviously thinks I was mean to Mum. Well I was, wasn't I?

It is weird about Mum though. One minute she doesn't do anything and the next I discover that she's up to aerobics and swimming and stuff and she's never even mentioned it. She's really into the choir and this homeopathy stuff – the woman who runs the clinic has become a friend of hers and they go off to the cinema together and everything. Don't exactly know what the homeopathy is meant to be doing for Mum but she seems much more relaxed and happier about life. She also seems to have better skin – sort of more glowing rather than grey.

And there are other good things at the moment:
1) Billy's more settled now that he's in The Grots. And he's so much more independent – he goes to Rory's and sometimes school on his own. Living here is different to anything else we've known but it's also a much more grown-up way of life for all of us.
2) Nicki's coming to stay this weekend – if we can find room amongst all the mess. Got so much to tell her!

Wednesday 15 March

Kim's forgiven me. Gave me a bit of a hard time about Mum but then she got over it. She told me today about Jake. Apparently he was getting too serious about stuff – wanting to see her more – but Kim said she liked things the way they had them: her going off to orchestra, Jake *playing footie, etc. Kim says it's best if they have their own friends as well as friends they see together. Wish I could be that cool about it all. But then I haven't even got a boyfriend, have I? I've seen Rob a couple more times at the leisure centre and at best he gives me a nod of acknowledgement. I've tried smiling back but it doesn't get me anywhere. What is it with boys? Why can't you be friends without having to go out with them? And I see Alastair at school a lot – but never when he's on his own. We don't have many lessons together or anything. And I never really get the chance to talk to him! Nothing is ever going to happen in my life!*

Thursday 16 March

Kim and Jake have made it up! Apparently Jake understood about Kim needing her space and they're back together again. I'm really pleased for her.

Came home from school today and the hall was full of tins of paint! Mum's gone bonkers and bought litres of the stuff because she said it was on special offer. I reckon there's enough to paint a battle ship. But anything is better than the shades of puke that we've got at the moment.

Nicki came down from London on Friday, straight from work. I didn't see much of her then though, because she went off with Mum to the Friday meeting of the diet club for Mum's weigh-in. Billy was already home when I got there and the pair of us just got on with our homework. That was one thing that Dad taught us: work first, then play, because if your conscience is clear then you'll feel happier at playing. It sounds a bit heavy but it's true – I mean who enjoys being at a party when you know that you'll have to wake up early the next morning to write that essay? No thanks. (Yes, so I sound like a swot – but that's how I am, OK?)

It was about seven-thirty when Billy and I met up in the kitchen (there was some progress: we now had one – unpainted – cupboard door and some shelves up, and the walls resembled a patchwork quilt where Mum had put up samples of paint all over the place to try them out on Billy and me – she was certainly more adventurous with her colour schemes these days than she'd ever been at the old place). We were both beginning to get hungry and raided the biscuit tin.

'I'll have the jammy dodger,' Billy grabbed it before I got the chance so I cuffed him lightly across the head.

'Oww!' he howled, rubbing his scalp. 'That hurt!'

'Oh no it didn't, Billy Boy!' I said as I joined in the scalp massage. 'Here – I'm going to have that chockie digestive at the bottom!' I dived to the bottom of the tin and grabbed the slightly battered biscuit from the bottom of the tin.

'Oh!' Billy tried to snatch it – but not very convincingly.

'Fair's fair, little brother. Finders keepers: you jammy dodger, me chockie digestive. Fancy a drink?' I flicked on the kettle.

'No thanks – you know I hate hot stuff. I'll have some milk though,' Billy went to the fridge. 'No – there's no milk, Hannah!'

My heart sank. After all the trauma we'd been through, Mum had started to get a grip on the house and stuff again. Or so I'd hoped . . .

'No way, Billy Boy. Here,' I pushed him out of the way. 'Let me have a look. You can never find things and they are always under your nose all the time.'

I had a good rummage round in the fridge and, unless the latest milk cartons had been carefully disguised to look like a bag of mushrooms, it seemed that Billy was right. No milk.

'We'd better go out and get some I suppose. Now, where's my purse?' I went out to get it from my coat that was hanging in the hall and then fished out some change. 'OK Billy, I'll see you in a minute.'

'Hannah, can I go and get it? Please?' Billy was so keen he almost snatched the money out of my hand. Obviously, the novelty of being able to be more independent for the first time in his life wasn't yet wearing off.

'OK, then,' I gave him the coins. 'You go and get the milk and I'll make my tea and see if I can find any more biscuits in one of the kitchen boxes.' Life was looking up . . .

* * *

It was gone eight-thirty before Mum came home with Nicki. We could hear them giggling as they came into the hall.

'Hannah! Billy!' Nicki gave us a combined hug. 'Quick – to the kitchen we go. We bring pizza! We bring wine!' She turned to Billy, 'We bring Coke! Let us feast and celebrate your clever mother losing another three pounds this week!' Nicki and Mum were certainly very jolly. I didn't understand it though, Mum usually came back from the diet club at about half seven or eight o'clock at the latest – so where had she been?

This time though, Billy got there first. 'Mum? Where have you two been? It's nearly quarter to nine! We're starving! And we didn't have any milk!'

Mum looked at her watch, gasped and pushed her glasses back up her nose. 'It's not, is it?' She giggled and put her hand over her mouth. 'Goodness, I'm so sorry. Quick, let's get the oven on to keep the pizza warm, and lay the table.'

I just stood there looking at the two of them, Mum and Nicki, as they giggled and bundled around the kitchen cluelessly. Billy though, wasn't going to give up. 'You haven't said where you've been, Mum!'

Mum looked at him and giggled again. Nicki giggled with her. 'Sorry, love – it's just that Nicki suggested we stop for a drink at that new wine bar up the road' – more giggles from them both. They were like naughty kids – 'and then we decided to go and get the pizza and there was a bit of a queue . . .' Even more giggles from the pair of them.

Billy looked at them and put his hands on his hips. 'Mum – have you two been drinking then?'

The pair of them giggled *again*. This time, it was Nicki who answered. 'Yes, Billy. Actually we have.'

We finally sat down to eat at about nine-fifteen.

'Don't you think your mum has done really well with her diet and everything?' Nicki poured some milk over her cornflakes. We were having a late, leisurely breakfast the next morning. All of us except for Billy who was, of course, off playing football with Rory on the common. They were taking part in a mini-league and I think Dad had promised to go and watch him but, diplomatically, none of us had mentioned that when Billy had left earlier on. 'I think she's looking great.'

'Yeah . . .' I put my spoon down and picked up my mug. 'She does.' I couldn't help myself smiling satisfactorily as I said it because it was absolutely true. She'd now lost nearly an entire stone and it was brilliant.

'Thanks, Hannah,' Mum smiled back and cupped her morning mug of Earl Grey in both hands. The sun was streaming through the dining room window and now that we'd managed to get rid of the dark green hessian which had made the room look, as Nicki had said, like the waiting room in a Chapel of Rest, the place was looking quite cheerful. Just like the kitchen, we still had a patchwork effect of sample paint colours on the walls (perhaps Nicki was going to tell us that this was a new way for people to decorate and that we ought to leave it like that permanently).

'It's nearly a stone! Only a few more pounds to go – I knew that my colleague Sheena was spot on when she suggested that you should write an article about that diet club. I knew that you wouldn't let yourself – or the magazine – down and that you would succeed. You know, I'm glad I went last night because it was really inspiring. I mean there were all sorts of people there, Hannah, of all sorts of ages who had such great stories to tell about themselves. Some of them had lost masses of weight. Others had just got round to getting rid of the pounds that had crept up on them over the last few years or so. But all of them looked happy and clearly felt good about themselves. Now I'm really looking forward to two things: seeing your mum when she reaches her target weight and then seeing her article when she sends it in for her copy deadline.'

Nicki was right, it was good that Mum hadn't failed the magazine – and more importantly herself.

'Now,' Mum yawned and stretched. 'I promised the old lady up the road that I would take her dog for a walk this morning. Either of you fancy coming with me?' She started to clear away her things.

'Well actually, I hope you don't mind but, if it's all right with Hannah, I wanted to take her out for the morning to that new discount shopping village. I wanted to buy her something for her new bedroom. Does that sound OK with you?'

'Sounds like a great idea to me!' I said and quickly began to clear away the rest of the breakfast things. 'How about you, Mum? OK?' I didn't want to upset her.

'That's fine, honey. Well, after I've walked this dog, I've got to pick up Billy from the football. So how about we meet up here for lunch? Say just after one?'

'No!' Nicki waved her hand, palm out, dismissively at us both. 'I've a much better idea than that. Let's meet up here at about one and then we'll all go and have lunch at that new wine bar – my treat. Good idea?'

'That would be lovely, Nicki. Only if you're sure,' Mum touched her friend's arm affectionately.

'Of course I am. It would be a pleasure. Now I'm going to quickly brush my teeth and get my bag.' Nicki looked at her watch. 'Come on, we'd better get a move on if we've got to be back here for one o'clock.'

It was great going with Nicki to the shopping village. I'd never been there before because it had only opened a couple of months ago and, as Mum said, spending money on things we didn't actually need wasn't really on until we'd finished doing up the house. We drove there in Nicki's car which is just gorgeous. It's small and sporty and – well, exactly like the sort of car that I want to drive!

On our way there (I navigated), Nicki and I had a chat about life. I told her all about Mum's progress.

'Well, it's great that your mum's doing all these things, isn't it?' It was warm and sunny and Nicki pressed a button on the dashboard and suddenly the roof started to slide right back. Wow!

' 'Course it is. It's just that, well . . . she's so secretive about some of it – and she seems to be doing so much herself, she doesn't need my help and yet, then again, she's so slow about other bits.'

'What do you mean?'

'Well. OK – those glasses! Mum's glasses are just awful, Nicki! She's been wearing them for absolutely yonks and they look so old-fashioned. They're so big for a start: she looks like that dreadful old bag on that soap on telly.'

'Hannah, your mum hardly looks like a dreadful old bag. Especially now that she's started to lose weight. But I agree that she needs to sort out her glasses.' Nicki paused as she looked left and right. We were approaching the shopping village and it was huge!

Once she was satisfied with her parking spot, Nicki and I headed off into the village. There was a huge map of the place just at the entrance. All the big shop names were there. This was going to be fun and I was glad that I'd brought my allowance with me! One of the good things about Dad living with Sally is that he gives us more allowance these days. ('Guilt!' says Gran.)

Saturday 18 March

Had a fabulous day! Went to the new shopping village with Nicki.

She treated all of us: she found Billy a huge sweatshirt; I got metres and metres of gorgeous sari fabric to make into a tent over my bed; and we found Mum a pair of brick-red linen jeans. Mum thought they'd be too small for her because they are a size 12 but they look cool. A bit tight but not for long and the colour looks great on her.

Nicki's going to go through my Design and Technology project tomorrow morning and she's given me a great pile of magazines about architecture. She's got a friend (I have a feeling he might be a kind of boyfriend) who's an architect. She's going to introduce him to me so that he can tell me more about it.

I also talked to Nicki about Mum's glasses and she's going to have a word with her. Nicki knows how to sort everything! She's going to persuade Mum to come and stay with her for a weekend and go shopping in London! Apparently they're going to a wedding of some old friend who's getting married for the second time. Mum wasn't

going to go as she hadn't got anything to wear. But now
she's going with Nicki and she's going to borrow some
clothes from the wardrobe at the fashion department on
one of the magazines! And Nicki's going to take Mum to
the hairdresser – and to the optician's as well now!

It's been brilliant having Nicki here this weekend . . .

It was Sunday evening and Mum had gone off for a swim –
again!

'Hi, Kim? It's me. How are you doing?'

'Oh fine thanks, Hannah. Jake and I have just been to a
concert at his brother's school. It was really good. Had a
good weekend with Nicki?' Things seemed to be all right
between Kim and me again after my balls-up at the
swimming pool.

'Yeah, terrific. We went to the discount shopping village
and got all these great things – you'll have to come over one
night next week and see them – and then we went out for
lunch at the new wine bar and then the cinema. Then, today,
Mum and Nicki went along to the garden centre and bought
loads of new plants for the garden. And Billy and I stayed
here and started to cook the lunch – it was actually fun.
Then Nicki had to go back to London after lunch. But you'll
never guess . . .' I told Kim all about the wedding and the
shopping trip to London and the visit to the magazine
wardrobe.

'Wow! Sounds great. Wish someone would do that for me!'

'Me too! Hey, have you done your homework?'

'Just about – well at least as much as I'm likely to have the brain capacity to do today anyway. Why?'

'Fancy going on the net and playing that word game again? Mum said I could for half an hour.' Kim and I had recently discovered this brilliant kind of Scrabble game that you could play with up to ten people at a time – people from all over the world who spoke English. It was really cool.

'OK. I'd better check it out with the old woman first though. Hopefully see you on screen in a couple of minutes then. 'Bye-ee!'

' 'Bye!' I raced to my Apple Mac.

CHAPTER 7

Monday 27 March

I know Kim thinks I'm a nerd but
I'm sticking to my revision timetable
religiously. I admit, playing with my
Mac is much more fun than revising for
Geography, but I feel dead chuffed when I can tick off a
subject on my list. Nice and organised.

Wednesday 29 March

Came home to find Mum up a ladder painting the dining
room ceiling. The house was in total chaos! Ghastly.

Friday 31 March

Read an article in today's paper about 'coping with
change'. It said you should make a list of all the good
stuff about the things that are changing and then
another one with all the bad stuff. So here goes:

Good things about moving to The Grots

I get to decorate my room

Billy's happier
Mum's getting it together
I can walk to Kim's
I can walk to school

Bad things about The Grots

Still visiting Dad at Sally's
It's a much smaller house
The builders are usually here at weekends
The mess they make

Tuesday 4 April

Kim and Jake are definitely a happy item. And I'm still single . . . but I did get to say 'Hi' to Alastair at lunch time today. He smiled at me! This time I smiled back.

Friday 7 April

Oh my God!! I've just got off the phone to Kim. She's asked me to go out with her and Jake on a date! On a blind date that they've fixed up with some boy that plays in Kim's orchestra! Eek! I'm excited and absolutely terrified at the same time! (I'd be more excited if it was Alastair of course.) Kim reckons this boy Tim (which is quite a promising name at least) is really nice. She said that if she didn't have Jake she'd fancy him herself! She even reckons he's cute to look at. I'm not so sure – I mean, if he's is nice, why hasn't someone else snapped him up already? Whatever, we're off to a film and out for pizza in a fortnight's time. It was meant to be this coming weekend but of course I can't go then, can I, because I've got to go to Daddy's house. It's so pathetic.

Mum's (she's lost another five pounds!) off to Nicki's at the weekend for her shopping expedition. (Wish that I could go.) Sally's bought tickets for Legoland. Legoland! I ask you! Even Billy's too big for that place. Anyway, there's no choice. It'll be great to see Dad and that – but we'll never get the chance to talk on our own, will we? And I won't be able to stay at home while they go off to Legoland because it isn't my home, is it? It's Sally's house and she won't want me knocking about there, will she? Not while she's not there.

Mr Pilkington was really pleased with my D and T project! It should give me a good mark in my final exam! He's suggested I write to the architects' practices in town to see if I can get some work experience at one of them during the summer holiday. Think I might give it a try.

I've made the tent thing for my bed. It looks fantastic. Kim says she's really jealous! I've painted the ceiling in my room white but mixed with this brilliant glitter stuff Mum found. Now I've got a very subtly glittery ceiling that sparkles gently at night when the light's on. It's cool.

The kitchen is now almost finished! All that's left to

do is to paint it and we've chosen all the colours and stuff. I must be getting really sad because I'm excited about a kitchen! Kim can't believe it, especially not after all the fuss I made before about even moving in here.

'There's Mum! There she is! Mum! Mum!' Billy was yelling at the top of his voice.

'Billy, please quieten down! Where's your mother . . . did you say? There? No,' Dad shook his head. 'No, that's not her, Billy. Sorry, son. She must be in another carriage.'

We were standing on the platform at the station as the Sunday evening train came in from London. Mum had been with Nicki as planned but, not as planned, Mum's train had been delayed just after it had left London. She'd rung Dad from her mobile (it was really awful because Sally answered the phone and looked really shocked. She didn't say anything to Mum and just passed the phone to Dad – she didn't even say anything to him! She just handed the phone over. I'm not certain but I think her hands were shaking as she did it too.) Mum told him that she wouldn't be home when she thought she would, so please would he tell us so that we wouldn't expect her to be there when we got home. In the end, the train was so delayed Mum rang again and Dad said he would bring us to meet her at the station. I'm not sure Sally was that pleased about it, but there wasn't much she could do because Dad just decided for some reason that that's what we'd do. Anyway, we'd been there for about twenty minutes before the train finally limped apologetically into the station.

'Mum! Mum!' Honestly, you'd have thought that Billy hadn't seen Mum for a month rather than a weekend. Billy had seen someone he thought was Mum in the first carriage which had sped past us and had shot to the end of the platform. Dad appeared to be convinced that it wasn't Mum and I hadn't even seen her – or whoever it was – so I couldn't say a thing either way.

'Come on, son,' said Dad, putting his arm around Billy's shoulder. 'She must be up this end of the train. Let's go up here.' So we started to walk up towards the back end of the train.

There were people all over the platform and piling off the train. I was surprised to see so many people on a Sunday evening but I suppose that the train was so late that, like us, people were coming to meet people that would otherwise have made their own way home. I looked as far ahead as I could see but I couldn't see Mum amongst the crowd anywhere. We knew she hadn't missed the train because she'd rung us from it. So where was she? Billy was looking really worried, poor kid. It was at times like this that you remembered that he genuinely wasn't much more than a baby. I think it rubbed home to Dad as well because he put his arm tighter round Billy's shoulder.

'Hello! Hi!' It was Mum! We all looked eagerly in front of us. Where was she?

'Mum! Mum?' Billy had pulled away from Dad and was running ahead of us.

'Billy! Hannah! I'm here!' Mum's voice was coming from behind us – we all turned round at the same time.

'Mum?' And there she was. She was wearing the jeans that Nicki and I had found at the shopping village (they were now just a perfect size on her) and a denim-blue jumper which I didn't recognise. She looked different. She looked great. Actually, she looked fantastic.

Billy ran up and threw himself at her. They bear-hugged each other. I joined in as well.

'Hi, darlings, how are you? Golly, I missed you two!'

'We missed you too, Mum!' Billy's pleasure at seeing Mum was transparent. I sincerely hoped that I wasn't making quite such a juvenile berk of myself! Then he looked a bit guilty and gave Dad a sideways look. 'I mean we've had a great time with Dad and Sa – and s-s-tuff. But we missed you too.'

'Of course you did, darling,' Mum gave Billy another bear-hug and then she turned to Dad. 'Thank you for bringing them to the station and coming to meet me.' She smiled at Dad who just stood there with his mouth open. There seemed to be a delay before he spoke – almost as if his brain was trying to engage gear.

'Umm, yes, fine. Yes, no problem. It's OK. No problem.'

He was flustered! Yep – he was flabbergasted! He just stood there gaping at Mum. And I'm not surprised because she looked just great – she really, really did! I mean she wasn't just wearing this new outfit which looked really good on her but she'd had her hair cut *and* she was wearing new glasses! Her hair was really glossy and thick looking with a sort of trendy reddish tinge to it – and much shorter. The glasses were these really chic ones: all sort of small and with thin silver frames – you know the ones like you see in the latest Calvin Klein ads? On top of that she was wearing make-up. Not much – but she had lipstick on that matched her jeans and her cheeks were glowing. I cannot tell you enough how good she looked.

It was obvious that Dad was pretty shocked to see her looking like that. And it was obvious that Mum enjoyed Dad being like that. *Looking* at her like that.

'Come on,' she said, turning away from Dad and back to us. 'We'd better get going home. I don't know about you, but I'm feeling peckish and I've brought some delicious fresh soup with me from Covent Garden.'

Mum went to pick up some of her bags and Billy and I helped her – I noticed she had some carrier bags and there was an enormous hexagonal-shaped box as well. Then we turned round and headed for the ticket office and exit from the station. Dad followed on behind. He sort of tried to take one of the bags but there weren't enough of them to go round really. He walked along behind us in a kind of semi-detached sort of way. I got the feeling he was uncomfortable.

83

'Right, we'll be off then.' Mum smiled at Dad again. 'Thanks for looking after the kids and waiting for me. Sorry about that delay. Come on you two, say goodbye to Dad and we'll get going.'

'Can I offer you a lift?' Dad didn't seem to know how to say goodbye. But it must have been obvious to him that having Mum in the car with the three of us would be embarrassing to say the least. Mum's smile wavered a bit.

'Er, no. I don't think so, do you? Anyway it's only ten minutes' walk to our house. Thanks anyway.'

So we said our goodbyes to Dad (which was really awkward in front of Mum) and walked home. Walked home with our Mum who had a trendy new haircut and really cool-looking clothes. Cool.

We chatted as we walked. Billy and Mum and me. Nineteen to the dozen, Gran would have called it. Everyone wanted to get in first and it was difficult to get heard. Then we all got the giggles when we realised how silly we all were, and then Mum said, 'Come on. We're almost home. Let's get that soup on and heat up this delicious bread I've bought. I know it's a bit late and you've got school tomorrow but – well, it's not as if we do this every week, is it? That OK with you two?'

'Yeah!' Billy seemed to be ecstatic – he'd got Mum back and now he was being encouraged to stay up late as well.

' 'Course, Mum. I'll lay the table while you sort out the soup and stuff if that's OK?'

'Sure, Hannah.'

And we turned into our road. As we walked the last few paces I pondered on how weird (and good) it was: I mean once upon a time, there's no way Mum would have let us stay up even half an hour late on the day before school, under any circumstances. Now she seemed really relaxed about it. Phew!

Sunday 9 April

What a weekend. Legoland was dire . . . So boring. Sally and Dad weren't that comfortable with Billy and me and Sally kept jumping over puddles so she didn't get her pathetic shoes wet! We had a bit of a laugh with Dad though.

Mum obviously had a great weekend. They found an outfit for the wedding; had lunch in Harvey Nichols where all the trendies go; then Nicki whisked Mum to the hairdresser (a belated birthday treat!). They even bought a fantastic hat. Mum said some complete stranger came up to her in the shop and told her she looked so good in it she had to buy it – so she did! And she's got these great new Calvin Klein glasses – the real thing! – and some fantastic new make-up that came from the sample box at Nicki's magazine.

There was a sad bit, though. I think Mum met up with
some old mates – one of them is working on American
Vogue*! Think it made Mum think about the career that*
she left behind when she had me and Billy. But a job in
London's not possible for Mum, is it! Because of me and
Billy. Still, she'd got this freelance stuff she's doing.

'Hannah?'

'Yes, Billy?' Occasionally, Billy and I had our act in gear and managed to walk to school together at a fairly leisurely pace, rather than running along together or going separately. This Thursday morning was one of those occasions. 'What's up?'

'Nothing's up. I just wondered. I mean, do you think that now Mum's had her haircut and stuff, Dad might come and live in our house?' Thank goodness Billy didn't look at me while he spoke because I didn't think that I could look him in the eyes and reply without crying. I felt really shocked by what he said. I knew Billy missed living like a family but I didn't realise that he still missed it that much. I thought he'd realised that Mum and Dad (and us too really) had reached a point of no return – especially now that our old house was gone. I kind of choked at the back of my throat as I tried to think of something to say.

'Um . . . I don't think so, Billy. Sorry.' I tried to stroke his shoulder with my right hand but I don't really think that I'm that good at stuff like that. I'm sure Gran would say that I will be one day – she's always going on about women becoming mothers and developing this kind of sixth sense about all sorts of things almost overnight. 'Sorry, Billy. You see I think that Dad's happier now that he's not living with Mum, so I don't think he wants to come and live in The Grots.' The nickname that I'd given the house had kind of stuck – even Mum called it The Grots now. 'And I mean, look at Mum. If you think about how Mum's been lately – losing weight, going swimming and off to aerobics and the choir – you know. she looks a lot happier too, doesn't she? I mean she is happier, isn't she? Happier with work and really into the house. Off to London for weekends and then to that wedding next week. She'd never have done all that a year ago, would she? You've got to admit that she's doing some good stuff.'

'So Dad's not coming back to live with us, then?' Billy did look at me this time. I gave him a straight answer.

'No, Billy, he's not. Why don't you ask him? Get him to tell you himself?' I reckon Dad deserved to answer a heavy question like this, not me. And I reckoned that Billy deserved an answer from him.

'He's coming to watch the football match after school next week. Perhaps I will. And I might ask him if he'll buy me the new Man. U. strip as well!' Billy gave me one of his smiles – what Mum and Dad called his cheeky grins. Billy may have been down, but he certainly wasn't out.

Thursday 13 April

*I'm so confused. Mum's still on a high and I'm really
pleased for her. But I'm also irritated by it – although I'd
never admit it even to Kim! Mum's relied on me for so
long, and this reinvention thing was my idea. So how
come Nicki seems to have taken over and sorted out the
glasses and hair! I wanted to do that! Now I won't get
the chance! And it shouldn't be a problem, but I think I
feel a bit left out . . .*

CHAPTER 8

It was Saturday afternoon and I was beginning to panic. Tonight was the night for the great blind date! I'd already decided what to wear and stuff and I was going round to Kim's at seven-thirty. Then we were going together to meet Jake and Tim at the pizza place in the High Street. After that was the movies: we were going to see that new Leonardo film. I couldn't wait – but I was dreading it at the same time. I wanted to meet this guy Tim – but what if he turned out to be a dork? I was looking forward to seeing what this new pizza place was like – but supposing I made a complete fool of myself in the restaurant? I thought back to the Alastair incident – *and* the Rob one – and groaned.

I'd done all my homework and coursework already this weekend. ('Good grief, Hannah, can't you chill out a bit?' Kim had said.) Then I'd helped Billy to paint a mural on his wall (his bedroom was looking really cool: it was mostly black and dark blue and the ceiling is covered with these star things that Mum found that glow in the dark). It was a sort of abstract picture in different shades of blue and black.

Now I have to admit that, just like Mum had said, I wouldn't want to sleep in that bedroom myself but it still looked good and I could see that Billy really rated it. It was his patch and he'd chosen it all himself and designed the mural. I'd just helped him by scanning the mural into my Apple Mac and then working out a way to divide the picture up so that we could then put a grid on the wall and paint the pattern within it. I was really pleased with what we'd done. So was Billy.

But now what was I going to do until seven-thirty? I mean, of course I was going to have a shower and get myself ready – but that wasn't going to take me that long, was it? And I'm not one of those girls who can take hours over painting my nails and stuff. I wish. I ambled into the living room, perhaps I could watch a video or something. But Mum was in the living room working on the PC.

'Hi, Hannah. How are you doing?' She looked up at me and gave me a smile. She was wearing lipgloss. Even on a Saturday, she was wearing make-up. Boy had she changed.

'Oh, fine thanks.' I slumped down on the sofa. 'What are you up to?'

'Oh, I was just working on that magazine article for Nicki's friend. I've got to have it done for next week and they're sending a photographer along to the slimming club to take a picture of me and the others.'

'That's great, Mum. You've done so well at it and you look

really good.' It was amazing to think that she'd stuck with the diet so well and had achieved her target weight without too much of a struggle.

'Thanks, Hannah.' Mum gave me a smile and went to push her glasses up her nose. Only there weren't any glasses. She hadn't got her new trendy glasses on!

'What's happened to your glasses, Mum? They haven't broken, have they?' I couldn't bear the thought of her having got so far as to get round to having the new glasses for that to happen to them.

'No, love. I'm just not wearing them today, that's all.'

'But you're as blind as a bat without them. You can't see without your glasses – that's what you've always said!' What was she up to?

'That's true, I am. But you can see me, can't you?'

Mum laughed and gave me a smile. 'Yes, sweetheart, I can see you. It's just that I'm not wearing my glasses because I'm wearing my contact lenses and –'

'Contact lenses?' I was stunned. When had *my mother* been out and got contact lenses? This was amazing! 'But where – when did you get them?'

'Thank you, Hannah! Actually I got them earlier in the week. After I went to that optician's when I was in London it made me think about the option of being able to be without glasses again. I used to wear them before I had Billy but then I suppose I just got lazy and couldn't be bothered with all that disinfecting to keep them clean. Nicki wears lenses you know, and she was telling me about this new cleaning fluid that does all the cleaning in one solution. So earlier in the week I took my prescription along to the optician's in town – they're part of the same chain that I went to in London. And I'm going to pay for them with the money from this article I'm writing for Sheena. I've got to break my eyes in to getting used to the lenses, if you see what I mean, so that's what I'm doing this weekend. No problems so far. Now, I've got to do the finishing touches to this copy, and then I was going to work on my CV. What –'

'Your CV!? What are you doing with a CV? Since when did you have one of those?' What was my mother up to? One minute she sprung on me that she had contact lenses and now she was telling me that she had a CV. Mothers don't have CVs, do they? My mother certainly doesn't.

'Oh thanks, Hannah! You know I did have a career before I had you and Billy! I may have spent the last few years concentrating on you and . . . and your father' – she gritted her teeth as she said it, almost as if she was trying to remember what Nicki had said that last weekend she had come to stay at The Grots: "Don't get angry, get on with it" – 'but I have always worked, even if it has been part-time at the *Borough Star*. Only I've been thinking and doing some sums. Working at the *Star* is OK but it isn't exactly challenging, and anyway, it doesn't earn me an enormous amount of money. I've been thinking and talking with Nicki about it. You and Billy don't need me as much any more – I mean Billy's out with Dad now and you've been keeping yourself busy all day – and that's just at the weekend. You're at school all day during the week. You don't need me in the same way that you used to. And if I don't start earning some more money, how are we going to afford to do things like replace the car when it needs it and go on holidays?'

I knew that Mum had been really upset last summer because Dad had taken Billy and me off on a holiday to Spain for two weeks. I'd heard her on the phone to Gran about it and she was making it clear what bothered her about it: first of all the fact that Dad hadn't ever wanted to go abroad with us; all he ever wanted was to go on walking holidays or spend time at home so that he could work on the garden. The other thing that bugged her was the fact that she couldn't afford to take us on a similar holiday to Dad's – Dad and Sally's trip to Spain last year (and I think another factor was that Sally was with us) was exactly the sort of holiday that she wanted to go on with us – once upon a time with Dad too.

I was perched on the edge of the sofa as Mum chattered away. I could feel a lump in my throat and I fought back the tears. This was ridiculous. I should be feeling really pleased for Mum – her lenses were just what she needed. But I just felt so left out – Mum hadn't even mentioned wanting them to me. And as for a new career . . .

'Hannah – are you OK, love?' Mum lent forward and touched my knee.

I took a deep breath and pretended to itch my cheek as I wiped away my tears. 'Yes, fine.' I tried to smile.

'Hannah, love – what is it?' Mum came over and hugged me as I dissolved into sobs. I didn't want to cry but somehow I just didn't seem to be able to stop it. I hated not being in control. 'Shh, Hannah. It's all OK,' Mum was gently rocking me, like she used to. I hate to admit it, but it was such a comfort I didn't want it to stop.

'Oh Mum, I'm sorry,' I spluttered between sobs and a runny nose. 'It's just that I don't feel like I'm in control any more.'

'What do you mean, sweetheart?' Mum cupped my head in her hands.

'Well – everything's changing so much these days. The house, Dad, you – even Billy.'

'I know love, I know . . .' Mum hugged me tight and, without thinking, I wrapped my arms around her too. It felt good: safe and secure. Something I don't think either of us had truly felt for a while. 'Oh Hannah, my sweet. It's all right. I know everything's changed but you know, it's not all change for the worse, is it?'

Mum stood back and looked at me. 'I didn't mean to get at you. I don't regret the time I've devoted to you and Billy – not in the slightest. It's just that I've got to give this job thing a chance. I'm not that young, sadly, and I have to be realistic. Things have changed a lot in magazine publishing since I last worked full-time – all that new technology and things like that. I probably don't stand much of a chance, but I've got to give it a try or I'll regret it for ever. Listen, give me five more minutes on this and then I'll switch the PC off. I promised Mildred that I'd take her dog out for a walk. Fancy coming with me?'

Mildred was the old lady who lived up the road. The three of us had struck up a bit of a friendship with her since we'd moved in: she was a retired music teacher and had all these really interesting stories to tell about things she got up to during the war. Mildred was always out and about doing things with her mates in her car (even though she was in her eighties) but she didn't have any family left around here any more, and she'd recently had a hip replacement operation. So she was mobile, but walking her dog for long distances wasn't really on. Mum tried to take the dog out for a longer walk once a week.

'Sure, that would be good.' I stood up from the sofa and smiled at Mum. 'I'll just go to the loo and grab my coat. See you in a minute.'

I enjoy walking dogs (probably because we'd never had one so walking one is a novelty). And walking this one this afternoon would take up some more time and stop me from thinking about that blind date.

* * *

Half an hour later, we'd collected Mildred's dog (which for some strange reason was called Puddy) and were heading for the common. It was quite a mild day but it was grey and overcast. Still, at least it wasn't raining.

'Are you in this evening, Hannah?' Mum paused to let Puddy have a comfort stop up the side of a lamp-post.

'Er, no. I'm going out with Kim and a couple of other mates.' I didn't really mind Mum knowing about it but I wasn't really sure how I could actually tell her.

'Oh, anyone I know?'

'Well, Jake, Kim's boyfriend,' (Mum had never met him but obviously she knew about him because she knew Kim and Kim's mum) 'and a friend of Jake's.' In for a penny . . . 'Kim and Jake tell me he's really nice. In fact I think he's more a friend of Kim's than Jake's – she plays in the orchestra with him.'

'Oh, that's nice,' Surprisingly, Mum wasn't being very nosey about it. I'd have expected her to be really curious to know more – you know, probing me for more information and stuff. It was almost disappointing that she didn't seem to be bothered about it at all! 'So have you ever met him before?'

'Oh no. It's a kind of blind date.' There, I'd said it now.

'Hey, what fun! Nicki and I used to go on lots of those when we were teenagers. Hah,' Mum giggled. 'When I think of some of the dreadful boys that we used to end up with for an evening! Dear oh dear!' She giggled again – it reminded me of the night that she and Nicki came back tipsy. 'Sorry, Hannah. I shouldn't mention these things – I might put you off and I'm sure this boy will be really nice. Jake is, isn't he?'

'He's OK. Not my type but Kim likes him so that's all that matters.'

'Well I'm pleased that you're going out because I've been invited to a party tonight. It was rather unexpected – I only got the phone call about it this morning and I hoped you wouldn't mind me going. What with Billy staying at Dad's – I didn't want you to be on your own, and now you aren't going to be, so that's good, isn't it?'

My mother was going to a party! 'Where is this party?'

'Oh, it's being given by some of the people in the choral society. They have a get-together once a year so that we can get the chance to talk to each other. You know it's really strange that we rehearse every week but we only usually get the chance to talk to the people that we sit with rather than mix with the other sections of the choir. It's nothing fancy. But it should be some fun.'

'Yes, but where is it?' She hadn't really answered my question.

'In the town hall – you know, in the big function room? Is there a problem? Surely you and Kim aren't going to the same party? I didn't know we had any member that young, even though it would be nice to have them.' We were on the common itself now and Mum let Puddy off her lead. You could almost see a smile on the little dog's face and hear it saying 'Freedom!' It waddled in front of us, nose down and fat little dog's bottom wagging.

'No, of course not. I was just wondering, that's all. So what time will you be back?'

Mum tilted her head back and just laughed out loud. 'Hannah – you are so transparent! Isn't it the mother that's meant to ask the daughter all the questions? Aren't I meant to know where and when you are going out? Shouldn't I be asking you for the telephone number of this blind date's parents and whether he is going to bring you home and at exactly what time so that I can stand and twitch the curtains in the living room, half an hour in advance?'

I could see her point and it was funny really. But, actually, I'd have preferred it to be the other way around. I tried to giggle to make out I didn't care. 'Sorry, Mum.' I bent down and picked up a stick which I threw for Puddy. She was so plump she was like a cartoon dog that ran on the spot for a few seconds before it managed to propel itself forward.

'You don't mind me going out, do you, Hannah?' Mum linked her arm into mine and kind of shivered. 'Oh that's nice. Keep me warm. You don't, do you, Hannah?'

'Er, no – 'course not. It's just that . . . well, it's just that you seem to go out a lot more than you used to, that's all.' And she didn't seem to be that interested in me going out either.

'Well, that's true. Everything's just got a lot easier to manage since we moved – we've all made a new life, haven't we? And made new friends? I mean I really love singing with that choir. I know you probably think it's boring – except you used to enjoy singing in the school choir until you stopped it a couple of years ago – but I really enjoy the music, and the challenge of reading the music again. And I also enjoy going to a place where people don't know anything about me: there's no baggage to take with me. I'm just me – not a divorcee or a single mother or a sad lonely woman with a big bum. Just me. And people treat me as an equal. Like I said earlier: things have changed for us – but not really for the worse.'

I squeezed Mum's arm. 'I know how much you enjoy it. It's good. When's that concert you mentioned? The one you've been rehearsing for this term?' Mum had asked if Billy and I would like to go if we invited Nicki down again for the weekend. I'm not sure that Billy particularly relished the idea of a classical choral concert. But when Mum mentioned going out for a burger afterwards I think he thought he might suffer it!

'It's in three weeks' time. They are starting to sell the tickets at the next rehearsal. Would you really like to come? I spoke to Nicki the other day from work and she said she's definitely on for it.'

'Great. Yes – I'd love to come. And I'm sure Billy will enjoy it too. It'll be good to see Nicki again as well.'

'Good.' Mum looked at her watch. 'Tell you what. Let's take Puddy round the other side of the common and stop off to buy something for tea from that new baker's. I've got a few spare calories up my sleeve to eat today!'

So we did.

Saturday 15 April (afternoon)

I'm all organised for tonight and I've got half an hour to kill before Kim comes to get me. Had a sticky bun for tea – so I'm not hungry but I can feel my stomach rumbling. What if it starts making noises in when I'm with Tim? I can't handle another humiliation in front of a boy. Surely my luck's got to get better?

Went for a walk with Mum this afternoon – had a great chat. It was good to see her without Billy Boy around for once. I know Kim thinks I'm being stupid, but I've been feeling a bit left out of it with Mum changing so much and doing so much. She hasn't seemed to need me at all.

But talking today has made me think a bit. Mum's always been there for us and I know she always will be. But she does need to get a life for herself. I can see that now. Nicki said something the other day – I couldn't really get it at the time but now it's fallen into place. That it's not so much a case of re-inventing Mum as refinding the person she used to be – before she had me and Billy and of course all the business with Dad.

I reckon Nicki's right – and Mum's pretty cool really.

The door bell's just gone! That'll be Kim – gotta go!

Sunday 16 April

Last night wasn't that brilliant but it was OK. Tim was all right – perfectly harmless, though he did remind me a bit of that telly character: Tim Nice But Dim. Only not so stupid. In fact he's probably really bright but he didn't have very much to say for himself, even when Kim tried to get him to talk about his orchestra and stuff. Perhaps he's just a bit shy. Bit funny that– I thought it was meant to be girls who were shy. I'm sure Alastair wouldn't be. Still the film was good – so was the food. And it wasn't even that nervous-making to be in the restaurant because poor old Tim being so nervous made it easier for me. I don't think he's going to ask me out again. But I don't think I'll cry about it.

Got the distinct impression that Mum had a better evening than I did. She didn't get back till nearly midnight. Someone gave her a lift home too! I think it was a man – I had a peek out of my window, though I couldn't see much. But she sat outside in the car and chatted for ages before she came in. What was she up to!

Over supper that night, Mum asked me about my date.

'Oh, he was OK. But . . .'

'Never mind, love. I told you – I can remember going out with some right creeps. Anyway, there must be some decent boys at school, aren't there?'

'Well . . .' I blushed as I thought of the delicious Alastair. 'Well, yes but . . . they don't seem that interested in me.'

'How do you know?'

'They haven't asked me out for a date for a start!'

'Have you asked them?'

'What?' Was my Mum serious?

'Well, how do they know you like them if you don't tell them? Give the lads a chance! Go on – ask someone out!'

'No way, Mum!' And I blushed down to my toes at the thought of asking Alastair out. Boy – imagine my mum wanting to do something as up-front as that!

CHAPTER 9

Wednesday 19 April

Decided to immerse myself in my revision. At least without a boyfriend to distract me I can devote myself to improving my chances in the exams.

Tuesday 25 April

Even I'm getting bored with ticking off my revision lists. Went for a swim with Kim tonight and saw Alastair going to play five-a-side football. He's such a dish!

Monday 1 May

Finished the hall! I'm so glad Mum and I had that chat the other week. It's cleared the air a bit – at least she knows how I feel now and knows it's not just been Billy who's had a bad time. I still wish I could sort things more – you know, wave a wand to get rid of the house dust and the builders, and sort out Mum's job. The other thing I'd do is stop Billy and his mates from being a pain (the bad news about being walking distance from school is that Billy's boring little chums are often in the house mucking about in the way that only painful thirteen-year-olds know how). Oh, and I'd also work out a way how to feel comfortable about seeing Dad with his arm round Sally. It makes me want to puke.

Mum was quite serious about this job thing. She'd started to get all these newspapers and magazines through the local newsagent that she said were essential reading for anyone involved with magazine publishing. I'd looked through a couple of them and they seemed pretty dull to me: just lots of articles and photographs of people who worked in the magazine and newspaper world with stories about their latest jobs and new launches of magazines, that sort of thing.

I was in the living room watching a film with Billy on the telly (hooray, his mates had gone) when Mum was poring through a great pile of these things. She kept on shaking her head in disbelief and muttering things like 'Imagine her getting that far!' and 'Heavens! I haven't got any of those under my belt'. In the end, Billy asked her what she was up to.

'Oh I'm just looking at the moves column – you know, who's got a new job and where. That way you have an idea of the jobs that are going to come up in the vacancies columns in the next couple of weeks. But I don't think I've got a chance with any of these jobs. They're all so high-powered.' Nonetheless, Mum was using a highlighter pen to circle some of the ads.

'Oh.' Billy wasn't very impressed. When Mum had first explained to him, like she had to me, about needing a new job, Billy couldn't understand at all why she had to go from the *Star*. As far as he was concerned, she'd got a job and it fitted in with everything else, didn't it? As the last couple of weeks had unfolded, I'd got to realise that Mum moving on and getting a new job was a good thing – and it was the final part of her reinvention. She'd got back her figure, her looks and most of her confidence. Now all she needed was a great job and we would all benefit, just like she'd said. Even if it did mean that she wouldn't be home every day when we got in from school. But I don't think Billy had realised that the new job would affect him in that way.

I'd phoned Nicki in her office about Mum's job search one afternoon when I came home from school and Mum was still out reporting for the *Star*.

'Isn't it great, sweetheart?' she'd said. 'Aren't you so proud of her? I'm not sure if she's realised it yet, but she's really found her feet again. And you've helped her to do it, you clever old thing.'

'Yes, Nicki. But has she got much of a chance with these jobs she applying for? I mean she could just be getting her hopes up only to get them thrown back in her face. I don't know if she could cope with that.'

'Sweetheart, that is kind of you to worry about her like that. But your mum's a tough cookie, you know – look how she's survived the last few months and come up smelling of roses! I'm sure there will be some disappointments but then I'm sure there will be a job for her somewhere. You'll see. It may just take a little bit longer than she thinks. Anyway, tell me about those letters you wrote to the architects' practices – any luck?'

I'd written to all the practices in the area to ask if any of them could offer me some work experience in the holiday. 'No. I've only had three replies so far and they've all said that they haven't got the space and time for me to come in.'

'Oh. Never mind. Any others still to reply?' Even Nicki sounded as if she didn't know what else to say.

'Two.'

'Well, there you are, then. If you haven't heard within the week, I'd be tempted to send them a reminder letter. You know – perfectly polite and things but giving them a nudge and reminding them that you are serious about it. Sorry?' Nicki was talking to someone else. 'Hannah, hang on a minute, someone needs me. Just a tick.' Nicki put her hand over the receiver and I could only faintly hear her talking – it was just like she'd gone under water at the pool. 'Hannah, sweetie? Listen, sorry but I've got to go. Look, I'm seeing you in a week or so's time. Don't worry about your mum, she'll be all right. Anyway – we're off to the wedding together this weekend. And don't forget to write those letters yourself if you need to. 'Bye, darling.'

When Mum came home that afternoon there was a pile of mail for her. She opened it all as she sat down at the dining room table and drank a cup of tea (she was still on the homeopathic stuff). She didn't say anything as she read the letters. She just sighed and ripped three of them up and threw the paper in the bin.

I guess they were rejections for job applications . . .

Saturday 6 May

God, I've taken refuge in Sally's dressing room. I'm stuck in this place all weekend thanks to Mum going off to the wedding with Nicki. Dad and Billy are downstairs watching the footie and Sally's knitting. Aargh!

Mum's been gone since Friday and we're here until after lunch tomorrow. I might die of boredom before then . . .

Sunday 7 May

Home! Had a blazing row with Billy this morning because of his GameBoy. Dad went bonkers – he ranted and yelled at us. He even said he expected more from us. He's got a nerve! Sally just sat on the edge of her stool looking nervous. She looked as relieved as I felt when Dad said it was time to take us home. No one spoke in the car.

Mum was all smiles – she'd had a great time and it

*showed. But she forgot to take her camera with her so
we can't see what happened until Nicki's pics are in!*

Home sweet home!

'So. D'you hear any more from Tim?' Kim and I were
changing after one of our weekly swimming sessions.

'No. But then I never gave him my phone number so it's
not that surprising really!' I laughed. Kim laughed with me.

'Sorry about that, Hannah. He seemed like a nice enough
bloke at orchestra. I mean he's really sweet and helps me to
get my place and music sorted and everything. But he wasn't
exactly at the head of the queue, I don't think, when the
doses of charisma were handed out.'

'Not exactly.' We both laughed. 'He was nice enough
though. I mean he doesn't look like a moron or anything.
And he's not stupid or unkind. In fact, he could be a good
catch if he wasn't so, so, so . . .'

'Boring?'

'Exactly!' We laughed again. 'Well, at least there were no
embarrassing scenes or misunderstandings.'

'True. And I'm sure that he'll be just the same as usual at
the next orchestra practice. Got time for a hot chocolate
before you go?' Kim was tying the laces on her trainers.

'Yeah, good one. Let's go.' I opened the door of our cubicle
and led the way to the café that overlooked the pool. We sat
down at a table that was next to the deep end.

'So, what are you up to this weekend?' Kim brought the drinks over.

'Oh, it's the concert for the choral society on Saturday night. We're all going with Nicki. But you know that, don't you? Aren't you going? Surely you are – to support your mum and that.' I couldn't believe that Kim had forgotten about it.

'Oh, bum! 'Course I'm going – but I'd clean forgotten about it. Don't tell my mum I did though!'

'My lips are sealed.' I took a sip of chocolate. 'So did your mum go to this party with the choral society the other day?'

'Yeah. She said it was good fun. She certainly came home late!'

'I reckon they're dirty stop-outs these mothers of ours. They certainly seem to be having a better social life than us – well than me, anyway.'

'You're telling me. You remember I went away to stay with my dad the other weekend. Well I'm certain that my mum had someone to stay – you know, a bloke.'

'Don't tell me she let him sleep in your bed?'

'Hannah! Are you thick or something? Not in my bed, you moron – in hers. You know, he slept with *her*.' She took a sip of hot chocolate and put her cup down firmly on the saucer.

'You mean your mother had it off with some bloke?' I couldn't believe it.

'Hannah, keep your voice down for God's sake,' Kim hissed at me.

'Sorry, sorry. I didn't mean to shout. It's just that . . . well . . . your mum . . . some bloke . . . Wow.' I still couldn't believe it.

'You make it sound as if my mum's some old bag who isn't capable of pulling a bloke. Anyway, it wasn't *some bloke*, as you so delicately put it. It was – or at least I think it was, because I'm not entirely certain there was someone there – anyway, if there was someone there, I think it was this guy she's been seeing on and off for the last six months or so. I've got to sit next to him at the concert on Saturday.'

'Wow. Your mum's got a boyfriend?' I really couldn't believe it. Mothers don't have boyfriends – they have husbands. Or they're just mums.

'Well, I thought he was just a friend – you know, someone for her to go out with and that. But I've noticed he rings her quite often. And I really do think someone was staying in the house because Mum was all shifty when I came home. And I found a bloke's razor in the bathroom.'

'Bit of a giveaway, then.'

'Exactly.'

I took another slurp of hot chocolate and looked at my watch. 'Look, I've got to go – I've still got my Geography notes to get straight.'

'Sure.' We started to walk out towards the exit.

'Well. I'll see you tomorrow, Kim. And I'll look forward to taking a good look at your mum's boyfriend on Saturday. 'Bye!'

'Yeah, 'bye, honey!' And she was off.

Friday 12 May

Mum had another rejection letter in this morning's post. She really had high hopes for this one too. She even went along for an interview – two interviews – in London. She said that the letter said that they liked her but decided in the end to go for someone they already had working on the magazine. Mum's <u>really fed up</u> about it – really fed up. There was another one of the trade magazines in the same post and she didn't even bother to look in it to see what this week's jobs were. That's how depressed she is.

Even Billy noticed she was fed up and loaded up the dishwasher without being asked. Bless him! He even said how much he was looking forward to the concert tomorrow night – and he's been moaning about it for the last two weeks saying 'Do I have to go?' every time it's been mentioned.

I feel bad because there doesn't seem to be anything I can do to help Mum. Nothing I can do to make it better. I hate that. And to make it worse, I had a letter in the post today from the last architect's practice. They've offered me two weeks' work experience in the school holidays. I couldn't tell Mum about it though, could I? It would have been like rubbing salt into her wounds. So I've kept quiet about it.

CHAPTER 10

Nicki arrived on Saturday morning. I knew she could tell immediately that there was something up.

'Billy and Hannah. I need you to do something for me. I forgot to bring some things down with me. If I write you a shopping list, will you go out and buy the things?' She didn't give either of us the chance to turn her down – not even Billy.

So we just went with the flow, took the shopping list, the money Nicki gave us, grabbed a shopping bag and went. Nicki followed us down the hall to the front door.

'Now, Hannah' – she was talking in a low voice so that Mum couldn't hear – 'You should have more than enough money. So when you've finished with the shopping go off to a café and get yourselves something to drink – or an ice-cream or something. I want to get whatever this is sorted before your mum's concert tonight.' She squeezed my shoulder. 'You and I will talk later – either today or tomorrow.'

'Yeah – see you later.'

Billy and I did the shopping and then I announced to him that we were going to the Italian café round the corner from home. Billy had worked out soon after we moved in to The Grots that living so close to the café was no bad thing. Their ice-cream – award-winning stuff – was like nothing you have ever tasted.

'Yes!' Billy punched the air in his usual childish way and then raced me to the café. He'd practically made his order (three types of chocolate and then even more chocolate on top) by the time I arrived. I ordered a bilberry and blackberry sundae and then sat down to wait for our ices to arrive. Billy had chosen a seat just inside the window and was gazing out at the passing world.

'OK, Billy?'

'Yeah.'

We sat in silence for a minute or two. It was Billy that broke it.

'Hannah? Is Mum OK?'

Oh. ' 'Course she is, Billy. Why do you ask?' I was trying to buy time, wasn't I?

'Well yesterday. She was really upset, wasn't she, about that job thing. I mean why does she want another job? She's got one.'

'Well she's got *a* job, yes. But she'd like another one. One that's more interesting – more like the job she used to have before she had us.'

'Yeah, but why?'

'Well, for one thing, Mum needs to earn some more money, Billy. Then she can afford to let us have a bit more – you know holidays, new bikes, trainers . . . ice-creams like these.' In perfect timing, the ice-creams arrived on the table in front of us.

'Oh, I suppose.' We both just ate for a while and then Billy said, 'You don't think Mum doesn't want us around any more, do you?'

'Billy!' I put my spoon down. 'You berk! Why on earth? What do you mean?'

'Well . . . if she gets a new job we won't see so much of her, will we? Maybe she doesn't want to see that much of us – I mean she's got so many new things she does these days. Like Dad . . .'

So that was what he meant.

'Billy, you know perfectly well that Mum loves us and doesn't want us out of her hair. I mean look how much she doesn't like us going to Dad's for weekends,' (although I had to admit she was less bothered by us going there these days) 'and she goes to all the football matches that Dad doesn't make and all the rest. She wants us there at her concert tonight, for goodness' sake.' Why didn't Billy ask Dad these questions? Why did I have to sort these things out?

'But Dad left because he didn't want us any more. So Mum could too.'

'Billy, don't be so daft. Of course that wasn't the reason why Dad left home. Look – I don't know exactly what went wrong between him and Mum but you and me weren't the reason why Dad walked out. I'm sure of that. So should you be. And Mum is not going to leave us. You know how much she loves us. OK?'

'OK.' Billy carried on eating until he'd cleared his glass.

'Sure you're OK? Promise?' Fortunately, I still had a bit more ice-cream left.

'Sure.' Billy gave me one of his grins.

'Listen – have you tried talking to Dad about this? You know, why he left and stuff?'

'No, 'course not. How could I?' Billy look incredulous. As if Dad wasn't someone you could challenge. As if Dad wasn't someone he felt so sure of these days. Sad.

'Easily, Billy. I know he doesn't live with us, but he's still our dad. Try talking to him – telling him how you feel. I know he'd want you to.' I really hadn't a clue whether Dad would want him to or not. But I didn't see why Billy shouldn't.

'You think so?' Billy looked a bit perkier.

'I do. Come on . . .' I'd finished my ice-cream. 'Let's go and see what's happening back at The Grots.'

Phew. This was turning out to be a heavy morning.

Mum was certainly looking brighter when we got back. Nicki gave me a conspiratorial wink when I handed the shopping over to her – as if to say 'Don't say a word now, we'll talk later.' Mum and Nicki were busy preparing lunch and we sat down to devour it an hour or so later. We were having lunch early because Mum had to go off with Kim's mum for a final rehearsal for tonight's concert.

Not only did Mum look brighter but she sounded it too. We all chatted away easily while we ate.

'Did your mum tell you about the wedding then?' It had been last weekend that the pair of them had gone off to the famous wedding – Mum in her new contact lenses and the amazing outfit that Nicki had helped her to put together. They'd arranged to get changed at a house near the church, so Billy and I hadn't seen Mum in the complete outfit – we'd just seen the bits and pieces waiting to go off in the car with her.

'Well, Mum told us what a great time you had – and how your friend made a great bride. She was telling us all about the flowers and the marquee and how you all danced until the fireworks – they sounded great.'

'Danced *until* the fireworks? You mean she didn't tell you how she danced until one o'clock in the morning with her toyboy then?'

'What's a toyboy?' Billy asked with his mouth full.

Nicki laughed. 'Well . . . it's a man, a young man. At least, one younger than your mum and me.'

This sounded intriguing. Mum certainly hadn't mentioned dancing with any man to me – let alone a toyboy. I looked at her across the table and she was blushing. She gave me a funny little smile and giggled.

'Hardly a toyboy, Nicki!'

'Well – he was a good deal younger than us. And he fancied you like crazy!' The pair of them giggled and Mum blushed even more.

Nicki was serious! She really meant it when she said Mum had danced with some young bloke who had fancied her. You could tell by the way Mum was reacting! How could some bloke fancy my mum – especially some young bloke. I mean she was my mum, for goodness' sake. She was Billy's mum. Mums don't get fancied by people. But then I remembered that Kim thought that some bloke fancied her mum. What were all these middle-aged women up to? Blokes were meant to be there to fancy girls like Kim and me!

'I tell you, Hannah,' – there was no stopping Nicki now that she was in full flow – 'he was really good-looking too. He's the son of a friend of the bride's parents – not that young, but almost ten years younger than your mum and me. No one there fancied me, I might add! I ended up dancing the night away with our old friend Geoff and some sweet, but frightfully old, man who was a friend of the groom's parents. He was a real charmer but he must have been seventy years old if he was a day.'

'It was a good wedding, wasn't it?' Mum looked quite wistful.

'Yes. And I've got some great photos of us too. They're in my bag, here.' Nicki rummaged in her bag and brought out a packet of photographs. 'I collected them yesterday. Look, isn't this one terrific of your mum?' She handed a photograph to Billy.

'Hey Mum, you look . . . different . . .' Billy handed the picture to me. Mum was looking sideways at someone coming down the stairs. She was smiling a glowing smile and her face was framed with the fantastic feathers of the famous hat. Billy was right – Mum didn't look like Mum in the photo. And yet she did look like her. And she looked . . . wonderful. If she looked like that at the wedding, I wasn't at all surprised that men fancied her.

'Mum! Hey, wow! No wonder you had a good time last weekend. You never told me about your man! Was he nice?' I smiled at her as I passed the photograph over.

'Yes, he was. Very charming, very good-looking. And very good at chatting up women who were older than him! Now,' – Mum looked at her watch – 'I'd better be off because I told Kim's mum that I would pick her up and take her to the rehearsal. What are you guys going to get up to this afternoon?' Mum stood up.

'Oh, don't you worry about us.' Nicki waved her hand dismissively. 'We've got a restaurant to choose for this evening and – oh loads of things, including the rest of these photos to look at. Now, be off with you and have a good time exercising your vocal chords. We'll see you later.'

'OK.' Mum picked her car keys off the hook by the door. 'See you at tea time then. Our choir master said we'd be finished at about four. 'Bye!'

' 'Bye!' We all said it in unison as Mum walked out of the door.

After Mum had gone, we looked at all the rest of the photographs from the wedding weekend. It was funny seeing Mum at a do without us. There she was in the photos having a great time, looking like someone who didn't have a husband and kids – or rather someone who hadn't had a husband and kids. She looked independent, sophisticated – and glamorous. My mum had really changed over the last few months. *My mum* . . .

After we'd cleared up the lunch table, Nicki suddenly announced that she was taking us out.

'We've only got three hours and I've booked us in to the bowling alley in town. I haven't been bowling for years and I thought it would be good fun.' Nicki was incredible. Was there no event that she wouldn't consider? Apparently not.

We had a great time and were back only ten minutes or so before Mum.

We had tea when Mum got back and then she went straight into the new shower that had only been finished that week.

(The house was really getting together now.) Then we all got spruced up and changed before we set off in the car – Mum was getting twitchy about turning up on time and getting into her place in the choir stalls. Nicki drove us in her car and Billy and I sat in the back. It was a bit cramped because it wasn't exactly what you'd call a family car. We were almost there when Billy piped up, 'So who is this Carmen Biriani anyway?'

'I'm sorry, Billy?' Mum turned round from her seat at the front and looked puzzled at Billy.

'Carmen Biriani or whatever her name is. The woman you're singing about tonight. Who is, or was, she?'

Nicki laughed and Mum held back a giggle too. Even I, who wasn't exactly a musician, could appreciate the joke that Billy had unintentionally made. 'Carmina Burana, Billy. That's what you mean,' Mum giggled again.

'Carmina whatever she's called –' Billy shrugged his shoulders. 'Who is she?'

'It isn't a she, Billy. The music is called Carmina Burana and it's written by somone called Carl Orff. No one actually knows what the words are, Billy. The composer found them on some ancient manuscript and no one knows what language they are or how to translate it. But the music is really stirring stuff, Billy. It's incredibly exhilarating to sing. You wait tell you hear it.'

'Oh I see,' Billy seemed happy enough with that answer.

Oh, Silly Billy. He was so infuriating – and so great at the same time.

Mum disappeared as soon as we got to the church to find her place like she said. Nicki and Billy and I found our seats. We were sitting in the second row from the front and had a really good view of the orchestra as well as the choir. We all read the programme (Mum's name was there as a member of the choir) and then I started to look round the church itself. The windows were really amazing and I looked up into the roof – I'd been reading a book on architectural styles and I was trying to work out if I could date the building. I looked at the carving on the ceiling beams and then my eyes followed the columns as they came down to the ground level. The choir stalls were very ornate. And there was my mum sitting in one of them. She was talking to a man. I've no idea who he was but they were chatting away – obviously Mum knew who he was because she was smiling at him and even looking as if she was laughing at his jokes. I sat looking at the pair of them. I couldn't be sure, but I think Mum was flirting with him . . .

The audience rose to their feet to applaud the choir and their orchestra. Mum had been right: the music was exhilarating and you could see the singers and musicians smiling away happily at their success.

There was a great sea of people trying to leave the church at the same time and Billy and Nicki and I waited just inside the porch of the church for Mum to come. When she did she wasn't on her own – she was with the man I'd seen her talking to earlier. She was definitely flirting with him. And what was more, he was flirting back. And they were so engrossed that they practically bumped into us on their way out.

'Oh – Hannah, Billy.' She kissed us both. 'Did you enjoy it?'

'Yes – it was fantastic. Really professional.' I gave Mum a hug.

'What did you think, Billy?' Mum put her arm around his shoulder.

'Well, it was very loud –'

Everyone burst out laughing – including the flirting man. Then we realised that we were blocking everyone's exit from the church. We strolled out towards the car. Flirting Man came with us.

'Nicki – let me introduce you to Nick.' Nicki and Nick shook hands and then Mum turned to Billy and me. 'And these are my children, Hannah and Billy.' He shook hands with both of us.

'Hi,' we all sort of mumbled.

'Nick sings with the tenors.' Mum tried to get us out of our embarrassment but it didn't work that well.

'Well, we'll go and get in the car then.' Nicki kind of

ushered us forward. 'Nice to meet you, Nick – look forward to seeing you again some time.'

'Yes, that would be nice.' Nick smiled at Nicki and waved. ' 'Bye, Hannah. 'Bye, Billy. Maybe see you soon.' He smiled at us too.

'Yeah, 'bye.' We walked to the car and Nicki opened it with her remote zappper button. Then Billy and I piled into the back. Nicki had just started the engine when Mum and Nick came up alongside us. Nick opened the door for Mum.

'Well, I'll look forward to seeing you on Monday then. You're still on for it?' Nick was holding the door open as Mum got into the car.

'Yes – I'll see you there at about seven-thirty.'

'I'll look forward to it. 'Night.' Nick shut the door as Mum put her seat belt on. He waved at us from the pavement as we drove off.

He was obviously going to see Mum at the next choir practice. Except choir practices were on Tuesday nights. And Nick said he'd see Mum on Monday. Of course! They were going on a date!

My mother had a date!

After the concert, Nicki drove us to this restaurant and we had a really great meal. Mum was much more relaxed than she had been before Nicki arrived. She was chatting and laughing away with us all about the concert and telling us all about the conductor who was the choir-master. I must say I wouldn't have known it had happened until Mum told me about it, but she said there was a moment when the sopranos got a bit lost and missed their cue from the conductor. We couldn't see it from the audience but Mum said that the conductor stared all goggle-eyed at the sopranos and they were so startled it made them lose their place again. And then the altos (that's what Mum is) came in late and then he started to stare at them. Apparently he was staring so hard that he then forgot to concentrate on the orchestra so they mucked up one of their bits.

We were in hysterics with laughing because Mum was so funny the way she was telling us about it all and the way she was mimicking the conductor. At one point she laughed so much herself she was crying and couldn't speak! When she got her breath back she told us that she couldn't remember the last time she had so much fun.

Neither can I.

We all met at the breakfast table the next morning. 'Very spoiling' was what Nicki called it. 'I don't do this at home. Yum.'

Billy was the last one to sit down – we hadn't got back from the restaurant until about midnight and I think that he was a bit knackered by that. He soon perked up when he saw the food on offer though.

I wished we had enough time to have a proper breakfast like this every day. But I wondered if maybe Mum and Billy and I could start doing this every Sunday, because it was fun – as well as delicious – and it was nice to take the time to chat.

'I really enjoyed last night, Mum.'

'Did you, darling? I'm pleased. So do you think you'll come again to one of my concerts?'

'Oh you can count me in,' Nicki piped up.

'Yes – me too,' I said, looking at Billy and waiting for him to reply as well. He didn't – he was still too busy munching away at his breakfast toast.

'So what are we going to do today?' Nicki was cradling her coffee cup in her hands.

'Well, Mildred's dog needs walking and then I've got a new recipe I'd like to try for lunch – including a pudding. As Nicki's got to go straight after lunch, how about we walk this morning along by the canal and then you guys can come back and have creative ideas for the garden – and clear out that rather murky bit in the corner – while I cook. OK?'

'Sounds good to me,' said Nicki.

'And me,' I liked the idea of the canal.

'Oww – do we have to go out for a walk?' Billy whined.

'Yes!' we all said and laughed.

The walk was just the thing to blow out the cobwebs from our late night. It wasn't warm but it was one of those really lovely mornings when you can wear a jumper and enjoy the warm sunshine on your face. Even Billy seemed to be enjoying it, throwing sticks for Puddy to chase.

Mum banished us all from the kitchen when we got back – she wouldn't even tell us what she was cooking. 'Just go out and clear that patch for me you three – the food's a secret!' She laughed and shut the bottom half of the new stable-door that we'd had put on the back of the house.

We went outside armed with thick rubber gardening gloves – and some big plastic sacks to put the garbage in. The corner of the garden obviously hadn't been cleared for years.

'Right. . . .' Nicki was brandishing some secateurs. 'Let's get cracking!' She hacked away at the brambles. 'This is quite therapeutic!' she laughed. 'I think these brambles represent all the people who've given me a tough time at work this week!'

Billy and I busied ourselves picking up the debris.

'Nicki?'

'Yes, love?' She carried on snipping away.

'Is Mum all right about this work thing?' This was the first opportunity that we'd really had to talk about it.

'I think so, love. It's just that it's a tough world out there and of course, one of your mum's problems is that she's having to catch up on all the changes in information technology that have taken place over the years since she last worked on a London magazine. She's done very well though – reading up all those magazines and journals has brought her up to date on lots of the people and things. And actually, the *Star* isn't that behind with everything. She's been working direct on to screen already – so she's really pretty clued up.'

'But do you think she'll get a job? I mean that's what she really needs now, isn't it?'

I looked at Billy who was busy playing with an ants' nest he'd discovered under the brambles. He really was still a kid – and he was so engrossed in his ants that he wasn't listening to a word Nicki and I were saying.

'Oh, she will. Wow!' Nicki tugged on a particularly tough weed which finally gave up and popped out of the earth, throwing her backwards. 'Phew! Hannah there is one piece of good news for your mum – I told her about it yesterday morning while you were out. You know she wrote that piece for Sheena? Well, Sheena was very impressed with the way she handled the whole thing – that's why she's been doing a few more things for her in the last few weeks – and she's also setting up a sort of sister magazine to the main one. It's about health and fitness. She needs a chief sub-editor for it, and she's going to ring your mum tomorrow to see if she'll come in and talk to her about the job.'

'That's fantastic!' I could feel myself grinning from ear to ear.

'Well there's nothing definite about it, of course,' Nicki wiped a damp leaf from her nose with her arm, 'but let's say I think she's in with a chance!' Nicki was smiling broadly as well. 'So I've lent one of my suits to your mum – you know, just in case she goes for an interview in the next few days!'

'Nicki, you're brilliant!' I gave her a hug.

'Yes – but don't forget that it's your mum that will be brilliant if she gets the job. There're no favours in the magazine world – you get the job only if you're good enough. Now . . .' Nicki put down the secateurs and took off her gloves. 'That lunch smells good,' (lovely aromas were emanating from the top half of the stable-door) 'and the head gardener needs a cup of coffee. Perhaps the undergardener could get her one?'

'Sure!'

Sunday 14 May

Had such a nice morning. Bit sad when Nicki left. Mum made this absolutely scrumptious meal she'd been asked to test for one of her freelance articles. It would be great if she got the job Nicki spoke about.

Told them about the letter I'd got from the architect's practice. They were both really pleased and Nicki promised to keep sending me those architecture magazines.

Nobody mentioned Nick though. I wonder where Mum's going with him?

CHAPTER 11

'You don't mind me going out tonight, do you?' Mum was speaking to Billy and me at the same time. We were having tea.

'No, suppose not. I've got an essay to write for history and I daresay that Billy will watch the telly when he's finished his homework, won't you, Billy Boy?'

' 'Course – there's a Real Madrid football match on tonight!' Well, that settled that, didn't it? There was no way watching that on the telly was going to be more exciting than doing my History essay – so no diversion there then!

'So where are you off to?' I tried to make out that I wasn't really that interested.

'Oh, Nick is taking me to see that new Meg Ryan film at the cinema. We're going to the deluxe screen so we're going to be served some snacks in our seats! Actually, there is an ulterior motive too because I've been asked to write an article about the new cinema for the paper anyway.'

Work! How could I have been so stupid to have forgotten to ask? 'Did you hear about that interview, Mum?'

'Yes,' she smiled, 'actually I did. I'm going for an interview on Thursday. And I'm terrified!' She clutched her stomach as if to contain the butterflies.

'That's terrific, Mum!'

'Yes – it might be. So, I'm going up on the nine o'clock train and then I thought I'd have a quick snack with Nicki, do a bit of shopping and then come back on the four o'clock train. You two can keep yourselves amused for a bit after school, can't you?' She did look slightly worried – maybe even guilty.

' 'Course we will, won't we, Billy?' We'd have to get used to this anyway, if Mum got the job, wouldn't we?

'What? Thursday? Oh, I'm going to play softball with Rory – there's a new team starting up and we thought we'd see if we fancy it.' Billy took another mouthful of pasta.

'There you are then, sorted!'

As soon as Mum went out, I phoned Kim.

'They've gone off to the cinema!' I reported.

'I asked my mum about him – of course she knows this Nick bloke too because of the choir. She says he's really nice: a solicitor. Apparently, he was married but his wife died. Sad, eh? Mum doesn't think he's got any kids though.'

Well that was a relief. It was beginning to sound a bit like a real Meg Ryan film plot! And if Mum was serious about this bloke, at least I wouldn't have to get used to some ghastly kid like Billy that came with him!

'Did your mum tell you that she and my mum are going to start doing another aerobics class? It's called Legs, Bums and Tums – isn't that a scream?'

'Why on earth do they want to do that?'

'Mum says that they both want to get rid of their cellulite, you know?'

'Cellulite? What's the point? Mum's lost the weight and she's hardly going to be going around naked for other people to see it, is she?' How ridiculous!

'How do you know?' Kim giggled.

'Well – she's not going to go nude sunbathing, is she? So who's going to see her?'

'Maybe this Nick bloke,' Kim said.

'You what? Why should he –' and then it dawned on me what Kim meant. 'You don't think they're going to, you know . . . do *it*?'

'Who knows, Han,' Kim laughed. 'I think my mum does so why shouldn't yours?'

'Oh that's disgusting!' And we both burst out laughing at the horror of it.

Later in bed that night, way after Mum got back from the cinema (Nick came in for a coffee and he asked me about the work experience thing!), I thought about people as old as my mum doing it – you know, *having sex*. I wondered if they did all the same things younger people did? Kissing with tongues and stuff. But then I didn't really know what younger people did (except what I'd read in books and seen in films), did I? But the thought of my mum and Nick, of Kim's mum and her man . . . Euech!

I switched off the light and tried not to think about it.

Thursday 18 May

Mum had her interview today. She came back really happy and confident. She thinks it went well but says she'll just have to wait to find out. Apparently, she won't know until next week. She met with this Sheena woman and two other people who work on the main magazine. The sister magazine is going to be published four times a year – so if she got the job, she'd have time to work on the main magazine as well, doing articles and stuff. Mum seems really excited – I really hope she gets the job.

Mum brought back a catalogue from some shop called Island. There's a really cool trouser suit in there. She said if I like it, she'll take me to London one Saturday and she'll buy me the trousers and Nicki says she'll pay for the jacket as an early birthday present. I'd have to buy a top to go with it myself. Well of course I like it, so that's a deal!

Strikes me that if Mum's going to go to London regularly and pop into shops like Island, then things really will look up around here.

I came in from school today and had hardly had a chance to put my bag down when I was ambushed by Billy.

'Hannah! Hannah! Mum's got the job!' It was great news – but I couldn't understand why Billy was looking quite so pleased about it, bearing in mind how miserable he'd been about the idea originally.

'Mum, that's fantastic! Well done!'

'Thanks, Hannah.' We hugged each other.

'And Mum's going to buy me a new bike with her first lot of wages!' No wonder Billy was pleased – this boy was easily won over!

'Now Billy, I didn't say that – not quite!' Mum mock-strangled him. 'I said that we would see if we could change your bike before the autumn. That's what I said, didn't I?'

'Oh . . .' For a fraction of a second, Billy looked downhearted. Then he beamed, 'Actually, Hannah, she did say that!'

Mum told me the rest of the details. She was going to start in six weeks' time and Nicki had already spoken to her on the phone and told her that she was going to go with her to this dress-exchange place in London. It was some shop where you could get these bargain-priced suits and office clothes. The reason why they were cheap was because they were second-hand – but they were all designer-label stuff that was hardly worn. Nicki said that the reason it was there was because it was last season's styles, so these really rich women took it along to the shop to get it out of their wardrobes to make space for the latest fashions.

'Nicki says that if we choose well, and get classic styles, I could walk out of the shop wearing designer labels for the price of something from a high street shop.'

'Sounds great, Mum – can I come with you?' I wanted to be in on this final stage in my mum's re-invention.

' 'Course you can. In fact, I thought we could all go, Billy as well. Then we can go and get your trouser suit with Nicki.' (Good stuff!) 'And I thought we could take Billy to a specialist bike shop in London so we could decide which one we're going to save up for!'

'Yeah!' Oh Billy!

'So Mum starts in six weeks' time!' I'd given Kim a blow-by-blow account on the phone.

'That's brilliant. Congratulate her from me, won't you? I expect Mum sends her love as well – I'll tell her about it when I put the phone down. So are you having a special meal tonight to celebrate?'

'Well, we had a special sort of tea – you know, cream cakes and tea bread. But Mum's out with Nick now.'

'Again?' Kim sounded surprised.

'Yes. But they had fixed it up before she knew about the job.'

'She seeing a lot of him, then?'

'She's only just started going out with him, I suppose. He rings her a lot though.'

'Do you mind?' Kim was always up front.

'No, not really. He doesn't spend that much time with us and most of the times he goes out with Mum, Billy and me are doing other things anyway.'

'That's OK, then.'

'And Mum's found out about this brilliant new thing they're doing at the leisure centre. They only announced it yesterday – which is why we didn't know about it at swimming.'

'What's that, then?'

'Trampolining! It's on Friday nights and Mum's asked me and Billy to go along with her!'

'Trampolining? Wow! And you're going with your mum?'

'Yep. Can you believe it? Not that long ago, Mum wouldn't have gone out of the house on a Friday night – now she's going trampolining with me and Billy!' I could hear Kim's mum calling her.

'Look, honey, I've got to go. Supper's on the table – and you know how I like my grub!'

' 'Bye – see you tomorrow.'

CHAPTER 12

Monday 22 May

The start of two weeks' revision leave before my exams. I've arranged to meet up with Kim for an hour every day to relieve the boredom and give myself an inspiration break. And a good old gossip!

Mum's going around like a Cheshire cat. I'm really pleased for her.

Wednesday 24 May

I've got brainache . . .

Friday 26 May

Met Kim in the park today and Alastair was there playing football. He is so fit . . .

Sunday 28 May

Lunch with Dad and Sally. Sally's given me a denim duvet cover for my new-look room. Bearing in mind how disgusting her own house is it's quite cool really. I guess she's quite nice but I still hate her for what she did to Mum. Used my revision as an excuse to leave early. Why do I never get to see Dad on his own any more?

Tuesday 30 May
Less than a week to go before my exams start. Aargh!

Thursday 1 June
Couldn't find my History file today and then I discovered that I'd left it downstairs and one of the builders had used it to prop open the kitchen door . . . !

Friday 2 June
Went to the park again with Kim just in case Alastair was there like last week. He was! I swear he winked at me but Kim says I imagined it.

Monday 5 June
So nervous about my exams I threw up after breakfast. French and Human Biology today. Geography and English tomorrow. I'm so nervous I don't think I can hold my pen to write.

Thursday 8 June
Struck dumb by exams. No energy left to write this diary.

Saturday 10 June

No more exams now until next Thursday. Kim's got one on Tuesday though. I can flop around a bit this weekend. Seeing Dad tomorrow – Billy's staying there for the weekend.

Tuesday 13 June

Met Kim after her Italian exam. Alastair was in the same exam. He looked dead glum and didn't even look at me when he came out. Went for a swim and a hot chocolate with Kim. Dead fed up about Alastair because I thought maybe he did fancy me after all.

Monday 19 June

My last exam today! It's over – until I get the results . . . Kim's finished hers this afternoon so we've got two whole weeks to chill out before we go back for "taster" sessions of the courses we think we want to take up next year.

Wednesday 21 June

Rang up Dad at work today and asked if I could meet him at his office for lunch. It was Kim's idea. She said at least that way I could get to talk to Dad on his own. Think he was a bit surprised, but I've arranged to meet him on Tuesday.

Friday 23 June

Swimming with Kim. The sun was shining so we went to the open air pool. Saw some boys there who were larking about – we reckoned they'd just finished their exams too. Chatted to them a bit at the bus stop when we left. Typical – the bus arrived just as the ice was beginning to break!

Saturday 24 June

Mum went out again with Nick tonight! She's so happy at the moment and she looks really good. Billy and I watched a corny film on the telly with Julia Roberts. Actually, I really enjoyed it – Billy kept on laughing though. Baby boys will be baby boys . . .

Monday 26 June

Off to see Dad tomorrow. I'm beginning to wonder what I'm doing it for – I mean, now I think about it, what are Dad and I going to talk about?

Tuesday 27 June

Mad day! Mum in a state because it keeps raining and she wonders if they'll manage to finish painting the outside of the house before she starts at the magazine.

Met Dad at his office. It was weird seeing him there with all those younger people. Of course, Sally was there, over the other side of the office. She waved at me but I pretended I hadn't seen her. Stupid, I know, but I hated the way she was trying to show off to everyone. I wanted them all to know what she'd done!

After a while it wasn't that difficult to talk to Dad. We went to this really trendy restaurant and talked about exams and stuff. I told him about the architect's practice job. He asked me about Mum's job as well. Strikes me he was more interested than he should have been – who knows?

Anyway, I'm glad I went – he gave me some more money too! Bet Sally doesn't know about that!

Thursday 29 June
The bathroom's finished. Mum and Billy and I stood around in it grinning like twits! It's really trendy – now I know what good taste Mum's got!

Friday 30 June
Went swimming with Kim at the open-air pool again. No boys there. Haven't seen Alastair for weeks . . . The Star *gave Mum a farewell party today. They even wrote a little article about her and her new job. I was dead proud of her.*

Saturday 1 July
Took Billy shopping today and we pooled our cash (used

Dad's money) to buy Mum a new bag for work. It isn't a briefcase but it's a lot better than the daggy old carrier bags she used to use at the paper. We're going to give it to her tomorrow.

Sunday 2 July

Gave Mum the bag at lunch. She started to cry! We all had a big hug and it felt good (how corny!). I'm so proud of her – I could feel a lump in my throat and I almost cried myself. I think even Billy did.

Back to school tomorrow for my "taster" sessions. Should be fun.

Monday 3 July

Billy and I saw Mum off today at the station. Then off to school. I never thought I'd say it but it was good to see everyone. Went to a Classical Civilisation session. Couldn't believe my luck – Alastair was there and he sat behind me! We even had a conversation. He's so funny! I think he was flirting with me!

Wednesday 5 July

Did an English taster today – History yesterday. Unfortunately, Alastair didn't do either of them . . .

Mum loves her job – you can tell by looking at her, let alone speaking to her. She's got a kind of glow to her. She

*bought what Nicki called a new capsule wardrobe and
she chose some really smart colours that suit her
fantastically. Can't get over how much Mum's changed
in six months.*

Friday 7 July
*Day off today. Swimming with Kim. There's a disco at
the leisure centre tomorrow night and everyone's going –
hope Alastair's there.*

Sunday 9 July
*Disco was brilliant – I sort of danced with Alastair!!!!
Well, he was in a group of people and we were all kind of
dancing together. Swoon!*

*Mum's still seeing Nick. He came with us for another
walk on the canal today. He seems all right, really. His
brother is an architect and he said he'd get him to have a
chat with me about training and stuff – after I've been
on my work experience. Excellent! It turns out that
Nick's into bikes as well – so that's pleased Billy,
because he's lent him some video about the Tour de
France. (Personally, I couldn't think of anything more
boring!)*

Monday 10 July
It's a bit weird coming home to an empty house every

day. But at least Mum's home by six-thirty. Mum's so full of beans that she chats away while she makes supper – sometimes I struggle to keep up with her, she seems to have so much energy these days. And she hasn't put back any of the weight either.

We're off to stay with Dad on Saturday – he's taking us to Disneyland Paris for the weekend with Sally. It's a bit of a kid's thing really, but Sally said we could sneak off to the shops on our way back to the Eurostar. I'm not sure I fancy spending time with her, but she's trying, I suppose.

I think Dad was a bit shocked when he saw Mum last time. Seeing her looking so good and that. I looked at a photograph of me and Mum on my birthday last year. Now, admittedly it was a photo taken by Billy, so it isn't a great shot. But Mum is almost unrecognisable compared to how she looks now. It's a really good feeling – for her and me. We've re-invented Mum!

At breakfast the next morning, Mum asked what we were up to Friday night. Billy was going over to Rory's to play some new computer game. I told Mum about Jo's party – it's her sixteenth!

'Got a good date to go with?'

I blushed. Once upon a time, Mum would never have said that! 'No – 'course not!'

'Now, Hannah! What did I tell you? If you fancy going with a boy, ask him. Don't expect the world to come to your feet! Go on – there must be one boy you like.'

'Yeah, Alastair!' Trust Billy to blab! I gave him a kick under the table. 'Oww!'

'Ah!' Mum put her tea cup down and looked at her watch. 'Look, I've got to go in a minute. So, is this Alastair at school?' She started to put her things into the case Billy and I had bought.

'Yes . . . but . . .' This was so embarrassing!

'So – ask him out, Hannah! Do it today! Right,' (she gave us both a kiss on the tops of our heads) 'I'm off to work. 'Bye!'

Tuesday 11 July

I can't believe I did it. I happened to stand in front of Alastair in the queue at lunch today. And I just blurted out about Jo's party and asked him! And he's coming!

I've got a date with Alastair! I can't wait until Friday. Oh, he's so gorgeous . . .